THE HARDER THEY FALL

Clint followed Big Ed out into the hall, where Dillon was tending bar. He quickly decided the best way to handle a man the size of Big Ed when that man was intent on breaking something, or somebody.

"When's the blonde comin' back?" Big Ed was snapping at Dillon when Clint approached him from behind.

Dillon looked past the giant man at Clint and before Ed could react, Clint took the man's gun from his holster and cold-cocked him with his own weapon. He didn't want to risk denting his own gun on the big fella's head.

Cooley stiffened, turned and stared at Clint, then fell forward. Instead of trying to catch him, Clint simply stepped out of the way, and Big Ed hit the floor with a thud that shook the building.

"Hold this," Clint said, handing Dillon the gun. "If he wakes up hit him again."

"I don't want to kill him," said Dillon.

Clint sighed, "Then don't hit him in the same place I did."

DON'T MISS THESE
ALL-ACTION WESTERN SERIES
FROM THE BERKLEY PUBLISHING GROUP

THE GUNSMITH by J. R. Roberts
Clint Adams was a legend among lawmen, outlaws, and ladies. They called him . . . the Gunsmith.

LONGARM by Tabor Evans
The popular long-running series about Deputy U.S. Marshal Long—his life, his loves, his fight for justice.

SLOCUM by Jake Logan
Today's longest-running action Western. John Slocum rides a deadly trail of hot blood and cold steel.

BUSHWHACKERS by B. J. Lanagan
An action-packed series by the creators of Longarm! The rousing adventures of the most brutal gang of cutthroats ever assembled—Quantrill's Raiders.

DIAMONDBACK by Guy Brewer
Dex Yancey is Diamondback, a Southern gentleman turned con man when his brother cheats him out of the family fortune. Ladies love him. Gamblers hate him. But nobody pulls one over on Dex. . . .

WILDGUN by Jack Hanson
The blazing adventures of mountain man Will Barlow—from the creators of Longarm!

TEXAS TRACKER by Tom Calhoun
Meet J. T. Law: the most relentless—and dangerous—manhunter in all Texas. Where sheriffs and posses fail, he's the best man to bring in the most vicious outlaws—for a price.

THE GUNSMITH

270

THE BIG FORK GAME

J. R. ROBERTS

JOVE BOOKS, NEW YORK

THE BIG FORK GAME

A Jove Book / published by arrangement with
the author

PRINTING HISTORY
Jove edition / June 2004

For information, address: The Berkley Publishing Group,
a division of Penguin Group (USA) Inc.
375 Hudson Street, New York, New York 10014.

ISBN: 0-515-13752-9

A JOVE BOOK®
Jove Books are published by The Berkley Publishing Group,
a division of Penguin Group (USA) Inc.,
375 Hudson Street, New York, New York 10014.
JOVE and the "J" design
are trademarks belonging to Penguin Group (USA) Inc.

PRINTED IN THE UNITED STATES OF AMERICA

10 9 8 7 6 5 4 3 2 1

ONE

When Clint Adams rode into Big Fork, Montana, he wondered how anyone had even managed to find it, let alone name it. He guided Eclipse down the main street, around the rainwater-filled potholes, so the gelding would not snap an ankle. He stopped in front of a firetrap of a building where someone had scrawled the word *Saloon* above the door with something—perhaps a piece of charcoal. He dismounted, tied Eclipse to a remarkably steady hitching post, and entered the saloon. What he found inside surprised him.

Given the falling-down appearance of the place on the outside, the fact that the inside looked like a small replica of a Portsmouth Square, San Francisco, gambling hall was a shock.

He approached the bar where a grinning bartender in his forties said, "Yeah, everybody pretty much reacts like that."

"It's amazing," Clint said, looking around. It lacked truly ostentatious furnishings, like chandeliers or crystal, but the long mahogany bar had definitely been brought in from somewhere, the walls were covered with flocked

1

wallpaper and oil paintings—mostly of voluptuous naked women—and the tables, chairs and gaming tables were all first-class furniture.

"Here," the bartender said, putting a mug of beer on the bar. "First one's always free to help you get over the shock."

"I don't get it," Clint said, shaking his head and picking up the beer, "if the owner had the money for all this why didn't he at least put up a real sign outside?"

"I think he just gets a kick out of the way people react when they come in," the barman said, spreading his hand, "but to know for sure you'd have to ask him. That'd be Mr. Ordway."

"John Ordway?"

"You know him?"

"I know of him," Clint said. John Ordway had owned a lot of gambling establishments throughout the West over the years. Clint was surprised to find he owned this one, out in the middle of nowhere.

"Is he around?" Clint asked. "I'm just curious enough to ask him about it."

"Sorry, he's not here at the moment. He said he had some preparations to make. He should be back later today, though."

"Is there a hotel in town?" Clint asked, hopefully.

"There are a couple," the bartender said, "one here in Old Town, and one in New Town."

"New Town?"

"The main road curves around a little farther up, and there's a whole 'nother section of town."

"Newer than this one?"

The bartender nodded and said, "That's why they call it New Town. Me, I'd rather stay down here."

"Why's that?"

"More action," he said, "and the sheriff's office is in New Town."

Old Town or New Town, Clint couldn't believe there was much more to this mining town of Big Fork.

"Also, the hotel here in Old Town is cheaper."

"I see. I'll have to check both of them out. Would you happen to know if Dick Clark is in town?"

The bartender's eyebrows went up. "Mr. Clark? Sure, he's been here a few days, now. You here for the game?"

"I am, yes."

"Well then," the bartender said, "Welcome to town. My name's Ben Dillon."

"Clint Adams."

Dillon's eyebrows went up even farther.

"You're Clint Adams?"

"That's right."

"Well then, I guess you'll be staying at the Old Town Hotel. At least, that's what I heard Mr. Clark say to Mr. Ordway," Dillon explained. "You should just go over there and tell them who you are. Your bill is gonna be taken care of."

Clint finished his beer off and pushed the empty mug over to Ben Dillon.

" 'Nother one?" Dillon asked.

"Yeah, one more to cut the rest of the dust and then I'll check out the hotel."

Dillon drew another beer and set it in front of Clint.

"What's the hotel like?" Clint asked.

"It's got everything a hotel is supposed to have."

"Like this?"

"A lot like this."

"And why would that be?"

Dillon smiled and said, "Because Mr. Ordway owns the hotel, too."

"That figures," Clint said. "What else does Mr. Ordway own?"

"I work for him," Dillon said, "and even I don't know the answer to that. Mr. Ordway doesn't talk about all his businesses—especially not to his employees."

Clint looked around the place again. Even though the gaming tables were covered he could tell how well made and expensive they were.

"What time do the covers come off?" he asked.

"About the same time the girls come to work," Dillon said. "And that's about the time the miners get off work."

Clint looked at Dillon. He was fit, seemed smart, and from what he knew about Ordway, this bartender was probably more than just a bartender, and probably knew more than he let on.

"Is Clark staying at the Old Town Hotel?" Clint asked.

"Yes, sir."

"And does it have a dining room?"

"Oh, yeah," Dillon said, "a good one."

Clint finished off his second beer and set the mug aside. He stuck his hand out and Dillon took it.

"I'll go and see to my horse, and check the hotel," he said, as they shook hands. "What do I owe you?"

"Forget it," Dillon said. "If you're here for the game, both beers are on the house."

"Thanks. Do I have to go all the way to New Town for a livery stable?"

"Follow the main street around," Dillon said. "The stable actually marks the line between new and old town. You won't be able to miss it. You'll also pass the hotel along the way."

"Thanks, again," Clint said, "and I guess I'll be seeing you around."

"It was an honor to meet you, Mr. Adams."

"Just call me Clint," he replied, and walked out.

TWO

Clint found the livery stable in the bend of the road and was able to look off at New Town. From what he could see, there wasn't much difference between Old and New Town, but he'd take a walk later to take a better look. He'd passed the Old Town Hotel, as Dillon had told him, and it pretty much matched the saloon in appearance.

"Beautiful horse," the livery man said, stroking Eclipse's neck.

"Yes, he is," Clint said. "Take good care of him for me."

"I sure will," the man said. He was well over sixty, tall and thin as a rail, but he seemed extremely fit. He had the scarred hands of a longtime horse handler, but they were powerful-looking hands. "This is the best animal I've ever had in my stable."

The livery was pretty large, with plenty of stalls, more than half of which seemed empty. The building itself had some age to it, but like the man, was sturdy.

"This looks pretty large for a town like this," Clint said.

"It was just expanded a while back to accommodate the people who are coming for the game."

"Ah," Clint said. "I couldn't tell."

"They used old wood to do the addition."

"What about the stable in New Town?"

"It's smaller, but it was built with new wood."

"Tell me something," Clint said. "Is this place owned by John Ordway?"

"Why would you ask that?"

"I'm here for the game," Clint said, "and to meet with Dick Clark. Is Mr. Clark's horse here?"

"Oh, yeah," the man said. "His horse is in the back on the left."

"So you don't know if Ordway owns this place," Clint asked, "or you're not saying?"

"I, uh, well, yeah, he owns it," the man said. "No harm in tellin' you, I guess."

"Tell me something," Clint said. "How long has New Town been in existence?"

"Only a year or so," the livery man said. "Used to be just one part of Big Fork, but the mines didn't play out the way folks thought they would and they started adding to the town."

"Riding in you'd never know there was another part to town," Clint said. "Why don't they try fixing up Old Town, getting the holes out of the street, fixing some of the buildings?"

The man shrugged and said, "I guess I don't know the answer to that, mister. I better see to your horse, now. He needs a good rubdown and some feed."

"Okay, thanks," Clint said. He collected his rifle and saddlebags from his saddle and allowed the old horse handler to take Eclipse into the building.

● ● ●

When Clint walked into the Old Town Hotel he saw that the money invested in the place had been spent on the inside, as with the saloon. Behind the new-looking front desk was a young clerk in his late twenties, looking freshly scrubbed and barbered.

"Good day, sir," the young man greeted. "Can I help you?"

"My name is Clint Adams," Clint said. "I understand you have a room for me?"

"Yes, sir," the man said, snapping to attention. "We've been expecting you. I can help you with you bags—"

"I don't need help, thanks," Clint said. "I just need my key, and a bath. Do you have tubs?"

"We have two, sir," the man said. "I can have one filled for you right away. Hot or warm?"

"Hot," Clint said, "as hot as you can get it." It would probably warm down some by the time he got to it.

"I'll take care of that, sir," the clerk said. He turned and took a key from a wall peg. "You've got room two, sir. Overlooks the front street."

Clint had seen when he entered that the front rooms had a small roof just outside the windows.

"I'll need a room overlooking the alley, with no access to the window from outside."

"Um, those rooms ain't as big, sir," the clerk said. "I was told to give you one of the bigger rooms—"

"What's your name, son?"

"Sam, sir."

"Sam, I'll tell your boss that you tried to give me a bigger room and I asked for another," Clint said. "You won't get into trouble for giving me what I want, I guarantee you."

"Well . . . okay, sir." He turned, replaced the key and took another one. "Room five, sir."

"Thanks. Have that tub ready, will you? I'll be down in a few minutes."

"Yes, sir. I'll see to it."

Clint turned to go to the stairs, then turned back. "Can you tell me who is in room one?"

"That would be Mr. Clark, sir."

"And is he in his room now?"

"No, sir, I don't think so."

"Okay, thanks, Sam," Clint said. "I'll see you in a few minutes."

"I'll have your bath filled," Sam promised, "and you'll have a fresh bar of soap."

"I'll look forward to it," Clint said, and started up the stairs.

THREE

After checking his room to be sure he was satisfied with it—he was—and taking his bath—which he was also satisfied with—Clint took that walk around New Town to see just how much newer it was. In truth, it didn't look all that different to him. The streets were still filled with rain-filled holes, and although the buildings were built of newer wood there really weren't that many of them, and they weren't that sturdy-looking. At best, Big Fork's New and Old Towns simply looked like two mining towns that had been pushed together into one.

Clint walked past the sheriff's office during his first walk through New Town, so on his way back to Old Town he decided to stop in and see who the sheriff was and what he was about. It also paid to check in with the local law when he was going to be in town for more than a day or two. Most lawmen did not like that kind of surprise.

As he entered the sheriff's office—one of the newer buildings in that part of town—he passed another man on the way out. He was young—mid-twenties—and was wearing a deputy's badge.

"Excuse me," the deputy said, as they almost bumped.

"No problem," Clint said. "Is the sheriff in?"

"He's right behind his desk," the young deputy said. "Name's Fenton, Enos Fenton."

"Thanks."

"No problem."

The deputy continued on, apparently not curious about who the stranger in town was. Clint entered and closed the door behind him. The lawman seated behind the desk looked up and said, "What'd you forget, Denny—" then stopped short when he saw Clint.

"Sheriff."

"Can I help you?"

"I just rode into town a few hours ago," Clint said, approaching the desk. "Well, I think it was town—it was Old Town, actually—"

The sheriff made a waving motion with his hand and said, "Forget all that. As you've probably noticed, there ain't a whole lot of difference between the two. As far as I'm concerned Big Fork is just Big Fork." He stood up, revealing himself to be of extraordinary height, with lots of chest and shoulders. He appeared to be in his forties, and Clint wondered how his weight would hold as he aged. His mustache was salt-and-pepper and covered his mouth entirely, and the hair on his head was thinning, but peppered just the same.

"Name's Fenton," he said, "Sheriff Fenton." He put his hand out and Clint grasped it. For a big man he had a firm, but not overly so, handshake. Clint read that to mean very little ego.

"Clint Adams."

Fenton stopped his handshake for a moment, the nodded, shook Clint's hand once again, and reclaimed his hand.

"Now I see why you felt the need to check in," he said. "I appreciate it."

The two men stood there for a moment, regarding each other.

"I suppose it's the game that brings you here?"

"Word sure seems to have gotten out about a private game," Clint commented.

"I generally hear about whatever's going on in this town," Fenton said, "or the county. I don't know how far and wide the word has spread beyond here."

"I don't know anything, yet," Clint said. "The only person I've talked to so far is a bartender name Dillon. Oh, and the livery man and the clerk at the Old Town Hotel."

"All employees of John Ordway."

"So I understand."

"Are you here as a player . . . or in some other capacity?" Sheriff Fenton asked.

"The buy-in for this game is a little beyond my reach," Clint said.

"Some other capacity, then."

"What my part will be remains to be seen," Clint said. "I'll have to speak with Dick Clark."

"Well," the lawman said, seating himself once again, "I appreciate you stopping by."

"I suppose I'll see you in Old Town from time to time?" Clint asked.

"Every night," Fenton said. "I don't really admit there's any difference between old and new, but that end of town is considered to be our red-light district. Or—to put it another way—the other side of the dead line—not that we're anything at all like Dodge City or Deadwood."

"These mines," Clint said, "they're silver, aren't they?"

"In the beginning that's all they were," the sheriff said.

"Folks figured they'd play out soon enough, but then they started finding other ore in the mountains and the town started to get built up."

"How long have you been the law?"

"I've been here a year," Fenton said. "They put the word out lookin' for a lawman, and I think I was the only candidate for the job."

"Just the one deputy?"

"So far."

"Pretty young."

"And green," Fenton said, "but he'll learn. I got twenty years of experience to pass on to him."

"I haven't heard of you before," Clint admitted.

The lawman smiled and said, "I tend to keep a low profile."

"Probably a smart idea," Clint said. "Well, I'll see you across the dead line, then."

"Be nice if you was to keep out of trouble, Mr. Adams," Sheriff Fenton said.

"I couldn't agree more, Sheriff."

FOUR

Clint made his way back across the "dead line," to Ordway's saloon. The covers had come off the tables and he could see there was faro, blackjack and roulette. The place was about half filled and the noise level was such that he could still hear the little white ball as it bounced around on the roulette wheel. Even as he entered behind two miners, though, three more came in behind him. It wouldn't be long before the place was in full swing.

He made his way to the bar where he found the bartender, Ben Dillon, working with both hands. There were also three girls working the floor, and at the moment, one—a lanky, long-haired blonde—was getting a tray of drinks from the bartender.

"Clint!" Dillon said. "You're back. Beer?"

"Thanks."

"Stacy," Dillon said to the girl, "this is Clint Adams. He don't pay for nothin', understand?"

"Whatever you say, Ben," the girl replied. She gave Clint a sideways glance. "Pleased to meet you."

"You, too, Stacy."

She smiled and left with her tray of drinks. Dillon put

13

a beer in front of him, then moved take care of the miners who had entered before and right after him.

"Ordway back yet?" Clint asked when Dillon returned.

"Not yet," he said. "Don't know what's holdin' him up."

"What about Clark?"

"Him, neither."

"Did they go together?"

"Guess they did," Dillon said. "They had some details to take care of about the game, I think."

Clint frowned. He was in Big Fork in response to a telegram from Dick Clark, a gambler he had known for some years. He knew about the game, and figured to find some of his good friends competing there, like Luke Short and Bat Masterson. Clark had asked him to come early so they could discuss his part in it.

"When is the game supposed to start?" Clint asked.

"In three days," Dillon said. "I don't think they're expecting players to start arriving for two days, yet."

"They'll drift in little by little," Clint predicted. "Might be some here, already."

"You playin'?" Dillon asked.

"That hasn't been decided, yet," Clint said. "It's another detail to be straightened out."

Clint was sure he had the skill to play, but the only way he'd be able to do so was if someone else put up the five thousand dollar buy-in.

"Well," Dillon said, "looks to me like there's mostly miners and locals in here right now. I ain't seen any other strangers in town but you."

"Maybe they're staying somewhere in the new section of town," Clint suggested. "I have to tell you, I took a walk over there and it doesn't seem all that different."

"What's mostly different is the attitude of folks who

live in that section," the bartender said. "They think they're better than everybody who lives over here."

"And why's that?"

"Beats me," Dillon said, with a shrug. "Seems to me some of them work side-by-side in the mines. How can one be better than the other one? I don't get it."

"Sounds like a good question."

Another girl came to the bar for drinks. She was a brunette, shorter and bustier than the blonde.

"Andy, this is Clint Adams. He's here for the game, and he don't pay."

Andy gave a full-on look rather than the sideways look he got from Stacy. She studied him, and he liked the bold look in her eyes. She also seemed older than the blonde, probably on the other side of thirty.

"The famous Clint Adams?" she asked.

"The only one I know of," he said, looking down at her cleavage.

She put her hand out and said, "Glad to meet you."

Clint shook hands with her. She retrieved her hand and picked up the tray full of drinks. "Maybe we can get better acquainted later."

"That sounds good," Clint said. "I'll look forward to it."

She smiled, then turned and went to serve her drinks. Across the room Clint could see the other girl, a redhead who was as slender as Stacy, but not as tall—or short—as Andy.

"That one's Trudy," Dillon said, meaning the redhead. "The boss wanted to hire a blonde, a brunette and a redhead."

"Looks like he did a good job," Clint said. "They're all pretty."

"And talented."

"I'll take your word for that for now," Clint said. "What's happening with dealers?"

"What do you mean?"

"I assume, with a game this big, that Ordway and Clark will be bringing in dealers."

"I don't know about that," Dillon said. "I'm just servin' drinks."

Clint had a feeling that Dillon was more than a bartender to Ordway, but liked to maintain that he "just served drinks."

Clint decided not to press the issue.

"I think I'll walk around and take a look at your operation," Clint said. "How about another beer for the trip?"

FIVE

Clint's impression of John Ordway had always been that he ran a straight operation. If Dick Clark was joining with Ordway to run the largest winner-take-all poker game ever run outside of San Francisco, that was even more of an indication that Ordway ran a straight game. Clint knew Clark, but he also knew that Clark and Luke Short were good friends, and Luke always vouched for Clark's honesty.

However, he did spot one dealer who wasn't exactly running his blackjack table on the up and up. As soon as a player won a few hands in a row the dealer would halt his momentum by dealing from the bottom.

By the time Clint got back to the bar his beer mug was empty.

"Another?" Dillon asked.

"No, thanks," Clint said. "You've got a bad apple in the bunch."

"Huh?"

"One of your dealers is a cheater."

"What?" Dillon asked. "Which one?"

"Table in the back—where Stacy is serving drinks now."

"That's Ed Brown."

"How long's he been working here?"

"About a month, I think. What's he doing?"

"Dealing bottoms," Clint said. "Whenever a player wins a few hands in a row he stops him cold."

Dillon leaned his elbows on the bar.

"And that's bad?" he asked. "Is he pocketing any money?"

"No, but—"

"And he's saving the house money?"

"Yes, but—"

"Then what's the problem?"

Clint stared at the man. "He's cheating."

"For the house," Dillon replied.

"It's still cheating," Clint said. "When you run a place like this, you have to run it on the up and up."

"Even if people are beatin' us, and takin' our money?"

"The house wins in the end, Dillon," Clint said. "Every time."

"Every time?"

"Without exception, so there's no need to cheat."

"I see." He pushed himself off the bar and went to wait on some more miners who had just arrived and were demanding whiskey.

Obviously the bartender was not a gambler and didn't understand the difference between winning by cheating and winning without cheating.

That wasn't something Clint was going to take the time to try to teach him, but he found it odd that such a man would be working for John Ordway.

He turned back to the bar to survey the room again. Clint wondered where Ordway and Clark were going to run the game. If they ran it here they'd have to close to the miners, and then where would they go? To a saloon in New Town? Wasn't Ordway afraid of losing some of his regulars during that time?

While he was standing there Andy came over to collect some drinks and stood right by him.

"Hello, there," she said.

"Hi, Andy."

"It's Andrea," she said. "In case you were wondering. I saw you checking out the operation. What did you think?"

"Everything looks top of the line."

"Except the dealers, right?"

"What do you mean?"

"Come on, I saw you watching Ed Brown's table. You know that he cheats."

"How do you know?"

"I've seen lots of dealers, Mr. Adams."

"Clint."

"Are you going to tell Mr. Ordway that you spotted him?"

"Why haven't you told him?"

She laughed. "And why would he listen to me? I'm just a saloon girl. I think you're the one who has to tell him."

"I will," Clint said. "It's not my job, but I hate cheaters."

"Even if they cheat for the house and not against it?"

"Obviously, you understand the difference," Clint said. "Your bartender doesn't."

"Ben? Ben's not a gambler."

"Well, I don't care who a cheater is cheating for. That man should not be dealing in a saloon."

Dillon came over and filled Andy's tray with drinks.

He stood and looked at them for a few seconds, and when neither of them spoke or moved, he moved on.

"Well," Andy said, picking up her tray, "I guess we'll be needing a new dealer soon. I'll see you later."

"See you," he said, and watched her walk away, giving her hips a little extra twitch just for him.

Clint finished his beer and put the empty on the bar. He waved Dillon off when the man started toward him. He wondered if he should try some gambling, but poker was his game and there was no table running. He played blackjack on occasion, but it held no interest for him tonight. Maybe some faro . . .

Before he could make a move, though, the bat-wing doors opened and Dick Clark came walking in. Clark was a tall, slender, pale man who stood ramrod straight, a holdover from his days in the military during the Civil War. His skin looked ever paler in contrast to the dark whiskers he sported.

"Well, it's about time," Clint said to himself.

SIX

Clark looked around the room, spotted Clint and walked over to him. Clint knew him to be in his mid-to late-forties but his slender build and pale complexion combined to make him look older. He had a dark coat on over an equally dark suit.

"Clint," Clark said, putting out his hand. "Sorry I wasn't here to greet you."

"I've been trying to entertain myself," Clint said, shaking his hand.

"They haven't charged you for anything I hope."

"No," Clint said, "not since I introduced myself."

"And you got all set up at the hotel?"

"I'm fine," Clint said. "All settled in."

"Have you eaten anything?"

The question surprised Clint, because he hadn't eaten anything, and he suddenly realized he was hungry.

"Now that you mention it."

"Come on," Clark said. "I know a place where we can eat and talk in private."

"Where's you partner, Ordway?"

"He's not here?" Dick Clark asked as they headed for the door.

"I thought he was with you."

"No," the gambler said, "I was running my own errands. I'll introduce you to him tomorrow. For tonight let's just conclude our own business."

They left the saloon.

Clark led Clint into New Town to a small café on a side street. It was run by a small man in his sixties who apparently waited the tables and did the cooking. He greeted Clark by name and allowed the gambler to pick his own table, since the place was empty. It was past dinnertime, and Clint wondered why he hadn't noticed before that he was hungry.

"Mr. O'Brien makes the best steaks in town," Clark said, removing his coat and hanging it on the back of his chair.

"I'll go with that, then."

"Two steaks dinners, then, Mr. O'Brien." Clark sat opposite Clint, who had seated himself so he could see the door and the windows.

"Comin' up, Mr. Clark."

"Coffee?" Clark asked.

"Definitely," Clint said.

"A pot, Mr. O'Brien."

"Yes, sir."

"He already knows you by name," Clint observed, as the waiter walked away. "How long have you been in town?"

"Been here about a week, putting things together. And I need to correct you on something."

"What's that?"

"John Ordway and I are partners in this poker game

only. Not in his saloon or in any other of his establishments."

"Okay."

"Sorry," Clark said. "Don't mean to be so sensitive. You know I usually like to run my own operation."

"I know that."

"Or else pick my partners," the gambler continued.

"Like Luke."

"Exactly."

O'Brien came back with a pot of coffee and two cups, poured them full and left.

"I need this," Clark said, and drank half the steaming cup down before refilling the cup.

"Dick," Clint said, "I have to ask, how did you pick this place for the game?"

"No distractions," Clark said right away. "And Ordway made a good case for using his place."

"Doesn't he have other places?" Clint asked. "Like in Denver? Or San Francisco?"

"See what I mean? Too many distractions in places like those. Big Fork was a perfect choice for a game of this magnitude."

"If you say so," Clint said. "It's your game."

"Yeah, it is," Clark said, staring into his coffee cup.

Clint waited, and when Clark didn't continue he said, "Dick?"

The gambler started, as if yanked from some sort of reverie.

"Sorry," he said, putting his cup down. "I'm tired. Did a lot of riding today."

"Are all your preparations done?"

"Pretty much," Clark said. "Now we just need to wait for the players to begin arriving."

"What are you going to do for dealers?"

"Ordway is supposed to supply them."

"Subject to your approval, I hope."

"Yes," Clark said. "Why?"

"Well . . . ! I looked things over tonight, and he's got at least one dealer who's cheating."

"Stealing from him? Ordway will kill him."

"He's not stealing," Clint said, and explained to Clark what he had seen.

"Doesn't matter," Dick Clark said, "cheating is cheating."

"That's what I said. What do you know about Ben Dillon?"

"The bartender? Not much. Why?"

"He didn't seem to care that one of the dealers was cheating. In fact, he didn't understand why I was upset."

Clark shrugged and said, "He's a bartender."

"I had the feeling he was more."

"Not that I know of."

"How could a man like John Ordway end up with a dishonest dealer?" Clint asked.

"I don't know," Clark said. "I guess we could ask him when you tell him about it."

At that point O'Brien returned with two steaming plates of steak and vegetables.

"Let's eat," Dick Clark said, "and then discuss our business over dessert. Peach pie still your favorite?"

Clint wasn't surprised that Clark remembered that. It was what made the man the fine gambler he was. He remembered everything about everyone he met.

"Yep, still is."

"Mr. O'Brien makes the best," Clark said.

"I'll look forward to it, then," Clint said, "after I've finished devouring this steak."

SEVEN

The steak dinner easily made Clint's list of top three, but when the peach pie came it went directly to number one.

"Wow," he said, looking at the old Irishman. "This is great."

"Thank you, sir," O'Brien said. "Mr. Clark told me it was your favorite. I will save the rest of the pie for you."

"Thank you, Mr. O'Brien."

"I'll fetch some more coffee."

As he went to do that Clint looked across the table at Clark, who had a piece of huckleberry pie in front of him.

"You had him make a pie just for me?"

"Just one of the incentives I hope will make you take this job, Clint," the gambler replied.

"What job is that?"

"First of all," Clark said, "I want you to know you're welcome to play in the game if you like."

"I don't think I can afford the buy-in."

"Maybe you can have someone back you," Clark said. "I believe we'll have several backers attending, and they might be interested in bankrolling more than one player to hedge their bets."

25

"Let's put that aside, for the moment," Clint said. "What was it you wanted me to do?"

"Security."

"You want me to arrange security?" Clint asked. "If you'd given me more time to line up some men—"

"No," Clark said, "I want you to be security. Just you."

Clint sat back in his chair.

"You want me to stand security for this game, alone?"

"That's right."

"Why?"

"Because I can trust you, and there's going to be a lot of money on the tables."

"You don't think you could trust men that I hand-picked?" Clint asked him.

"No offense," Clark said, "but I would only trust men who I handpicked—and I'm picking you."

Clint ate the last bite of his pie, washed it down with coffee and sat back again.

"There's more," Clint said, "isn't there?"

Clark hesitated, then said, "Okay, yeah. I figured letting it be known that the Gunsmith was standing security for the game would be deterrent enough to keep anyone from trying to hit the game."

"I'm the only man you'd trust with this?"

"Well, no," Clark said. "I'd trust Bat Masterson, but he's playing."

"Who else?"

"Well . . . Luke, obviously, but he's playing, as well."

"Okay," Clint said, making a quick decision, "how about this. I'll agree to the job, but if Bat or Luke are eliminated before the end of the game, I'll press them into service."

"That's fine," Clark said, 'but don't you want to know what the pay is?"

"I know you'll pay me well for this, Dick," Clint said. "There's no need to negotiate."

"Do you want the money in advance?"

Clint almost said no but stopped himself.

"Is Ordway putting up half the money?"

"He is."

"Okay," Clint said, "I'll take his half tomorrow, when I meet him. I trust you to pay me the rest when the game is over."

"You don't mind if I put it to John another way?" Clark asked.

"Whatever way you want is fine with me," Clint said, "but now we come to the question of the dealers again."

"What about them?" Clark asked. "Once we tell John about this dealer—what's his name?"

"Ed Brown."

"Ed Brown—once we tell John he'll fire him and we'll be fine."

"No," Clint said. "I want to interview all the dealers. I want the right to eliminate them if I feel they're a security risk."

Clark thought a moment and said, "I can get John to go along with that."

"Why don't I do that?" Clint asked. "The three of us can get together tomorrow and I'll outline all my conditions for taking the job."

"Fine," Clark said, "just don't mention the part about wanting his half of the money first."

"I'll leave that to you."

"Fine," Clark said. "Then we have a deal?"

"You and I have a deal," Clint said, "yes."

"Good," Clark said. "John will go along with everything you say. You were his first choice, as well. Have you ever met him?"

"No," Clint said, "we've never crossed paths."

"Okay, then," Clark said, "I'll introduce the two of you tomorrow morning."

"Where's the game going to be played?" Clint asked. "You're not going to close down the place, are you? This game might go on for days."

"I'll take you over there now and show you where the game is going to be," Clark said. "It's upstairs from the saloon."

"That building has a usable second floor?"

"Oh, yeah. It was built for that—sort of like the second floor Luke put on the White Elephant."

"What's with the outside, Dick?" Clint asked. "Why doesn't Ordway fix that?"

"He doesn't want the place to look too rich on the outside," Clark said. "He thinks it would attract the wrong element."

"There can't be that many people in this town, or that many people riding through."

"He thinks word will spread and people will come."

"So if they hear about it and come to see it, it makes more sense for the outside to be presentable."

Clark heaved a sigh and said, "Yes, to you and me. Not to John Ordway."

Clark paid the bill, saying that Clint was now on the payroll, and they left to walk back to the saloon. Clint put the collar of his jacket up, wishing he had a coat like Dick Clark's.

"You know, I've never heard much about Ordway's personality," Clint said. "This thing with the outside of the saloon . . . sounds kind of . . . odd."

"John's an odd man," Clark said. "He has his own ideas about how to do things—but then we all do."

"Your places have always looked good inside and out," Clint pointed out.

Clark lifted his arms and then dropped them to his side. "I don't get it either, Clint, but that's John. His places have always made money."

"Seems to me he's taking a chance with this one," Clint said, "what with the location, and all."

"He actually bought this place and fixed it specifically for this game. He wants to make it a yearly thing."

"That's odd, too," Clint said, "buying a place to have a poker game there once a year."

"I'll let you make your own observations about John Ordway when you meet him," Clark said. "I have enough trouble explaining my own attitudes."

"Well," Clint said, "there's a point I can't argue with. I have the same problem, too."

EIGHT

When they reentered the saloon, the night was in full swing. There were no spaces at the bar and all the tables were gone. Clint followed Dick Clark through the busy saloon, pausing just to exchange a wave with Andy. Clark led him to a stairway and then up to the second floor. There were several rooms up there, all filled with gaming tables, but Clark took him into the biggest room—which seemed to be as large as the saloon on the first floor— which was filled with green felt–covered poker tables with pockets at each chair for chips.

"This is the main room" Clark said. "If we have enough players we can always use the other rooms."

"That'd be a security nightmare," Clint said. "Two or three rooms? I'd have to sit in the hall the whole time. How many players are you going to have, anyway?"

"We've got ten tables in this room," Clark said. "That should be it."

"What're you playing?"

"Five card stud."

"Ten to a table, then?"

"Right."

"A hundred players, five thousand a man buy-in?"

"That's right."

"Half a million dollars?" Clint asked. "Winner take all?"

"Yes."

"Jesus," Clint said. "I can see some sore losers waiting outside for the winner. Why don't you pay for second or even third place, as well?"

"Winner take all is more exciting," Clark said, "and the best player wins."

"Or the luckiest player."

"Luck will get you to the final table," Dick Clark said, "but you're gonna have to be good to win."

Clint didn't reply. It was a matter of opinion and he didn't want to argue it. If the best player won, then Luke Short would be sitting with all the money by the end of the night.

Unless . . .

"Are you playing in the game, Dick?"

Clark hesitated, then said, "I'm not sure, yet. I'm not sure it would be ethical."

"Why not? You pay your money, you play."

"I'm hiring the dealers."

"Have Ordway do that. He's not playing, is he?"

"No."

"Or let it be known that I hired the dealers."

"Chances are I won't play," Clark said. "We'll be cutting the games, anyway."

"Each hand?"

"Yes."

"Then you'll make your money. Still, a half a million is a tempting jackpot."

"Tempting to you?"

"Sure," Clint said, "I'm human—but if I'm working for you and it's unethical for you to play, I guess the same would apply to me. Besides, I couldn't play and take care of security."

They stood there in silence for a few moments, each alone with their own thoughts. Clint looked around and saw with satisfaction that there were no windows.

"Let me see the other rooms up here."

"This way."

Both of the other rooms were small and would probably only accommodate three or four more tables each. If both rooms filled, the jackpot would get as high as nine hundred thousand dollars.

Both of those rooms had windows, so Clint said, "Have those windows boarded up."

"Even if we're not going to use these rooms?"

"They would still offer access," Clint said. "I don't want anyone coming up here who doesn't use that stairway from the saloon."

"Then you'll want to see the back stairway."

"Great," Clint said. "Show it to me."

It was a narrow stairway in the back that led down to the rear of the building.

"Close it off," Clint said.

"How?"

"Get a carpenter, have him board up the windows and then close off this stairway. He can build a temporary wall downstairs."

"Okay."

"This will be a nightmare for one man, Dick," Clint said when they reached the main room again.

"We'd feel so much better with just you, Clint," Clark said. "We trust you, and have faith in you."

"That's good," Clint said. "This'll probably be the first time I've seen Bat and Luke play where I'm rooting for one of them to lose early."

"It would probably be better if we didn't tell either of them that," Clark said.

"On that we agree."

"Let's go downstairs and have a beer."

"Lead the way."

On the way down the hall to the stairs, Clark said, "You met Dillon, how about the girls?"

"I've been introduced to two of them" Clint said. "Stacy and Andy."

"Stacy's something, isn't she?"

Tall, rangy blondes must have been Clark's type, because Andy appealed more to Clint.

"They're all pretty great-looking, Dick. Will they be working the tables?"

"We haven't decided whether to have drinks served or not—"

"Don't."

Clark stopped at the head of the stairs.

"Why?"

"Liquor and sore losers don't mix, Dick," Clint said. "Come on, you know that."

"We got a couple of players who like their whiskey with their cards," Clark said.

"Let them take a break and have a drink," Clint said. "Tell them it's a matter of security, and if they want to complain to someone tell them to see me."

They continued down the stairs and when they reached the bottom, Clark grabbed Clint's arm.

"No room at the bar," he said. "I have a private table in the back."

Clint nodded and followed Clark to the table. Their butts had just settle into the chairs when Stacy appeared asking if they wanted drinks.

Dick Clark had her trained already.

NINE

Dick Clark and Clint had two beers together and caught up with each other's lives, since it had been a while since they'd last seen each other.

"How long has it been?" Clark asked at one point.

"Five years?" Clint asked.

"Five," Clark said, "that sounds right . . . but where was it?"

They both thought a moment, then Clint said, "San Francisco. . . . no, Sacramento."

"Denver," Clark said. "Bat made four tens and beat Luke's full house."

"That's right," Clint said.

"He should never even have been in that hand," Clark said. "What luck!"

"That's what I was saying upstairs," Clint said. "Sometimes it's luck."

"But I won that game in the end," Clark said. "I beat both Bat and Luke. There was nothing lucky about that."

"If you say so."

Clark put his second beer mug down with a bang and leaned forward.

"Do you want to know why I'm really not playing in this game?" he asked.

"Sure," Clint said, "tell me."

"I'd win."

"You're sure of that."

"Positive," Clark said. "Why would I ever play if I didn't expect to win every time?"

"But you don't win every time."

Clark frowned, and at that point he decided to have another beer. Clint decided to go to his room and turn in.

"I want to get an early start in the morning," Clint said, standing up.

"I'll have one more and then do the same," Clark said. "Meet me in the morning at O'Brien's at nine for breakfast and then we'll come back here and see John."

"Okay," Clint said. He turned and found himself face-to-pretty-face with Stacy.

"Another beer, Mr. Adams?"

"Not for me, Stacy," he said. "I'll say good night."

Clint felt something move inside him. He decided to leave or else he might not get any sleep at all that night.

Clint couldn't fall right to sleep, no matter how tired he was. He was thinking about the game and all the money involved, and all the people that amount of money would bring to Big Fork—gamblers, backers, and criminals.

He was still thinking about it when there was a gentle knock on his door. A knock like that usually came from a woman, but the one time he didn't take his gun to the door with him he knew he'd regret it, so he slid it from the holster hanging on the bedpost and took it to the door with him.

"Who is it?" he asked.

"It's Andy."

He opened the door a crack, saw her in the hall and then opened it all the way.

"I'm alone," she said, "if that's what you're worried about."

He leaned his head out to look both ways, saw that the hall was empty, and breathed in her fragrance.

"You left without saying good night," she scolded him.

"And you came up here to say that?" he asked.

"Oh no," she said, "I came up here for much more than that." She put her hands against his chest and pushed him, putting most of her weight behind it. He staggered back and she entered, closing the door behind her.

"You and me had a connection today," she said, dropping her shawl from her shoulders. She was still wearing her dress from work, an off-the-shoulder blue that showed off her rounded shoulders and clear, milky skin. The darkness between her full breasts was an inviting mystery, and the smell of her was a heady mix of perfume, perspiration and her own natural musk.

"Tell me I'm wrong and I'll leave," she said. "But if I'm right, I'm taking off my dress."

"You're not wrong," he said.

"Well," she said, "if you'll drop your gun, I'll drop my dress."

"Deal," he said.

He didn't drop the gun, because there was a chance it might go off, but he did lean down and place it on the floor. Andy slid the dress down from her shoulders and let it fall in a heap at her ankles. She was naked underneath and he feasted his eyes on her opulent curves. Her breasts were round and heavy, with large, brown, inviting nipples. She was not a skinny girl, and as she turned so he could look at all of her, he saw her flaring hips, her chunky buttocks, full thighs and a veritable jungle of black hair down between her legs.

"You are a beautiful woman, Andy," he said, in awe.

"Some men like Stacy," she said. "You know, the long, lean type? Not you?"

"Oh, no," he said, "not me. I like my women to have some substance to them."

She laughed throatily and asked, "You mean some meat?"

"That's exactly what I mean."

"Well, honey," she said, "if that's what you like, you're in luck."

Over at the saloon, after closing, Dick Clark walked to the back where John Ordway had his office, knocked and entered. Ordway, a large, florid-faced man in a black suit, was seated behind his huge desk, which he had originally bought in St. Louis, and which he now shipped to whatever new establishment he purchased and intended to run for any length of time.

"So?" Ordway asked. "How did it go?"

"He agreed," Clark said, sitting heavily in a chair across from Ordway.

"You said he would."

"This game is a big lure," Clark said, "even for someone not actually playing in it."

"Any players arrive yet?"

"Not that I know of," Clark said. "At least, nobody I know."

"When do I meet Adams?"

"In the morning after breakfast."

"Good. Did we get him cheap?"

"No."

Ordway scowled.

"Well, he better be worth the money."

"He wants half up front."

"My half, right?"

Clark didn't answer.

"That's all right," the other man said. "It's not a problem. What else did he say?"

Clark informed Ordway about the adjustments Clint wanted concerning the windows and new walls.

"Okay, we'll get a carpenter in here tomorrow," the big man said. "What about you?"

"What about me?"

"You decide if you're gonna play?"

"I'm not," Clark said. "Wouldn't be right."

"It wouldn't be right for you to play and win, Dick," Ordway said. "If you don't play what are you gonna do for the duration of the game, watch?"

"That's a good point," Clark said, "but if I play I'm going to play to win."

"And what are the chances that you will win?"

"Very good."

"Well then, maybe I should back you."

"That really would look bad," Clark said. He stood up. "I'm tired. I'm going to bed."

"Where's Trudy?"

"Damned if I know," Clark said. "Must have gone home."

"Maybe she's upstairs."

"Maybe."

Because of the large rooms upstairs there was only space for one living quarter and Ordway had it.

"Did you show Adams my living quarters?"

"No," Clark said. "He would have made us board the windows."

"Good. I don't want anyone messing with where I live."

"As long as we keep your door locked there won't be a problem," Clark said.

"You taking Stacy with you?"

"No."

"Why not?"

"Good night, John."

Ordway laughed and said, "Good night."

Clark went through the saloon and Dillon let him out the front doors, then locked them behind him. He took a deep breath. Clint had been the last piece, and now he was in place.

Tomorrow it all started.

TEN

Andy's breasts were incredibly firm in Clint's hands as he lifted them to his mouth so he could suck her nipples. She moaned and put her head back and he sucked them until they were hard. Her hands went to his belt, then, and she worked until she had his pants down around his ankles. He'd already taken off his boots, so kicking out of his pants and underwear was no problem. His shirt came next, and then he slid his hands down her back to cup her buttocks and pull her to him. His rigid penis was trapped between them and her skin was amazingly hot against his.

"On the bed, damn it," she said, pushing him again. "I didn't come here to play games."

She pushed him down on his back and then joined him on the bed, positioning herself between his legs. She took his penis in her hands and caressed it, drawing a moan of pleasure from him.

"How do you feel about aggressive women?" she asked, rolling his penis between her palms.

"I love them," he said.

"So it wouldn't shock you if I did . . . this?" She leaned over and took the head of his dick into her mouth. She

43

sucked it until it was wet and then let it pop free.

"No," he gasped, "that wouldn't shock me."

"So it wouldn't disgust you if I did . . . this?"

She leaned down farther and engulfed his penis in her hot mouth. She lowered her head until her mouth was flat against him, the entire length of him in her mouth. He lifted his hips as she began to bob her head up and down, suckling him, sliding her hands beneath him to cup his buttocks. Abruptly, she allowed him to pop free, and his penis prodded the air, pulsating and red.

"No, no, no," he said. "That doesn't disgust me."

"Good," she said, "because you taste like candy, and I love sucking you. I know some women don't do this, but I'm gonna do it all night. Is that all right?"

"As long as I get a turn."

"To suck me down there?"

"Oh, yes."

"Really?" she asked, surprised. "I haven't met a man before who likes to do that."

"Well, I love to do it," he said, "especially to a woman who tastes good—like you."

She smiled at him, fondling him again, and asked, "You think I taste good?"

"I know you do."

"How?"

"Well, for one, you nipples taste wonderful," he said, "and for another . . . I can smell you."

He was surprised when she put her hands over her mouth and blushed.

"You can . . . smell me? Down there?"

"Oh, yeah," he said. "You're wet, aren't you?"

"Oh, yes," she said. "Feel."

She straddled him and then rubbed her wet pussy up and down the length of him.

"Oh, yes," he said, "definitely wet."

Suddenly, he grabbed her between both arms, lifted her off him and put her on her back. He'd allowed her to push him around long enough. It was his turn.

When Dick Clark got to his hotel he was surprised to find Stacy waiting in the lobby.

"Stacy. What are you doing here?"

"I walked over with Andy," she said.

"Andy? Where is she?"

"She went upstairs to Mr. Adams's room."

"When was that?"

She shrugged. "Fifteen, twenty minutes."

"And you're waiting here for her to come down?"

"No."

"Then what are you—"

"I'm waiting for you, silly," she said.

"For me?"

She stood up, then gave the clerk a look until he turned his head the other way.

"You're too much of a gentleman to invite me up, aren't you, Dick?" she asked.

"Well, uh—"

"Is it all right if I invite myself?" she asked. "Or would that . . . put you off?"

"I don't think anything about you would ever put me off, Stacy."

"Well then, shall we go?"

Meekly, the gambler allowed her to lead him up the stairs to his room.

Clint kissed Andy's breasts, and then worked his way down her body, pausing to stick his tongue in her deep belly button. Finally, he was where he wanted to be and he worked on her with his lips and tongue. If possible she became even wetter than before as she squirmed beneath him.

"Mmmm," he said, pausing just for a moment. "I was right about you. You taste delicious."

"Oh, God," she said, grabbing his head, "don't stop . . . don't you ever stop doing that. . . ."

He went back to it and didn't stop for a very, very long time.

1

ELEVEN

Clint woke in the morning with Andy curled up against him. She had kept him warm all night long, and he hoped he had done the same for her. When he moved she felt him and reached an arm and a leg across him.

"You can't leave," she said. "I'm too warm."

"So am I," he said, "but I have to meet someone for breakfast."

She bit his shoulder and said, "You're not buying me breakfast? What kind of gentleman are you?"

He thought a moment, then put an arm around her and said, "Well, if you get up and get dressed you can come and have breakfast with us."

She looked up at him and asked, "When is breakfast?"

"Nine."

She turned her head and looked at the light coming in through the window.

"It's only dawn," she said, reaching down between his legs. "We have time."

"Yes," he said, spreading his legs, "we do."

She slid over him and mounted him, taking him deep inside of her. She began to ride him that way, her full

47

breasts pressed into his face. He bit them and squeezed them, moved his hips in unison with hers so that their flesh began to slap together audibly. His penis began to make a wet, squelching sound every time it came out of her. All the sounds began to mingle together as they moved faster and faster. She sat up and began to move up and down on him harder and harder so that her breasts began to bounce up and down, his eyes entranced by the nipples.

"Ooh, God," she moaned, reaching behind her to brace herself on his thighs. "Oh my . . . last night was incredible . . . and now . . . this . . . ooh . . ."

Her nails dug into his thighs but he barely felt it. She was sucking him with her pussy and that sensation was all he was aware of. He felt her begin to tremble and knew from last night's experience what that meant. She was close to her ultimate pleasure and he felt himself racing to meet her. Suddenly, he was exploding inside of her and she was bouncing wildly on him, biting her lip, still waiting for hers to overtake her, and when it finally came she pushed a fist into her mouth so that when she screamed it was muffled.

In the end, Andy decided not to go to breakfast with him, because she would have had to wear the same dress as the night before.

"And I need a bath," she said. "You go and have your breakfast and I'll see you later."

He kissed her and they parted in front of the hotel. He was about to head for New Town when he saw Dick Clark come down to the lobby with Stacy. He stepped aside so that Clark wouldn't see him, flattening his back against the wall.

"Are you sure you don't want to go to breakfast?" Clark asked the blonde.

"No," she said. "I need to get some sleep, and a bath. I'll see you later."

Much the same conversation he'd had with Andy. He assumed they'd had much the same kind of night, too.

Clark turned in his direction and stopped short when he saw him.

"Good morning," Clint said.

Clark looked embarrassed.

"Mind if we walk to breakfast together?" Clint asked. "I'm starved. I had a . . . stressful night."

"Yeah," Clark said, "mine was kind of strenuous, as well."

The two men exchanged a wry grin, then turned and walked to O'Brien's together.

"I didn't even invite her," Clark said, "she just showed up."

"Mine, too," Clint said. "We've got ourselves a couple of real aggressive women."

"I'm not used to that," the gambler said.

"Luckily," Clint said, "I am."

They had two plates full of eggs, potatoes and bacon in front of them, as well as a basket of warm rolls and a pot of O'Brien's strong coffee. It was the best breakfast Clint'd had in a long time.

"Is Ordway back?" Clint asked.

"Yes," Clark said, "I saw him last night."

"Did you give him my terms?"

"I told him you'd agreed to work for us," Clark said. "You can repeat your terms to him today. I'm sure he won't object to any of them."

"None?"

"I doubt it."

"What about you?" Clint asked. "Did you decide whether or not you'll play?"

"I don't think so," Clark said. "I can't convince myself it would be the right thing to do."

"I'm sure no one would think anything of it."

Clark smiled and said, "There's one in every bunch."

"Like who?"

"I'm not sure who's coming and who isn't," Clark said, "but Ben Thompson would be one. He's not a very agreeable fellow on his best day."

"You've got a point there—if he comes."

"Players, backers . . . they should all start arriving today."

"Including the others."

"Others?"

"Hangers-on, slackers . . . the scavengers."

"Oh, them. Well, they'd have to hear about the game, first."

"Somehow," Clint said, "they always manage to, don't they?"

TWELVE

After breakfast, Clark and Clint walked back to John Ordway's saloon.

"You have a key?" Clint asked.

"No," Clark said. "Ordway doesn't trust anyone that much."

"How do we get in?"

"We knock," Clark said. "Dillon will open the door."

"Does he live here?"

"Only Ordway does," Clark said. "That's all he had room for after he decided to add all the gaming rooms upstairs."

"Are you sure Dillon will be here?"

"He always is," Clark said, raising a hand to knock on the front door. "It's part of his job."

He pounded his knuckles on the door and almost immediately it opened.

"Good morning," Ben Dillon said. He pushed the batwing doors wide. "Come on in."

They walked in and Clint saw a man seated at one of the tables with a plate of breakfast in front of him.

"Dick," the man called out, "good morning."

51

"Morning, John. This is Clint Adams."

"Mr. Adams." Ordway stood up. Clint had not expected him to be such a large man. "Welcome to Big Fork."

They approached the big man and he and Clint shook hands.

"I've been looking forward to meeting you," Ordway said, "even before Dick and I discussed you doing security for this game."

"It is kind of odd that we've never crossed paths," Clint said.

"Please, have a seat, both of you. Coffee?"

"Sure," Clint said.

"Fine," Clark replied.

"Ben, some cups and another pot."

"Yes, sir."

They all sat and Ordway smiled. "What do you think of my operation?"

"Inside it's great," Clint said.

Ordway laughed. "The outside keeps people off balance. That's a gambler's edge, you know, keeping somebody off balance. But I don't have to tell you that. You've played in enough big games yourself."

"A few."

"And you've gambled with higher stakes than I have," Ordway said, "putting your life on the line. I'm sure when you're facing someone with a gun it's good to have them off balance."

"Definitely."

"There you go."

Dillon returned with the cups and a pot of coffee. He placed them on the table and left it to each man to pour his own, then retreated to the bar. Undoubtedly he was getting it ready for business that night.

"Dick tells me you have some conditions for us," Ordway said. "I'm sure you've outlined them for him and he's fine with them, but I hope you won't mind letting me hear them."

"Not at all," Clint said. "You'll be paying me, after all—at least half, as I understand it."

"You understand correctly."

Clint took a few moments to explain his conditions to Ordway, the main ones being that when it came to security he was the last word and that he would interview all the dealers for the game.

"That's fine," Ordway said when he was done. "I don't have a problem with any of that. I was planning on using my dealers, since they're already here."

"Well," Clint said, "then you have a problem already."

Ordway was lifting a forkful of eggs to his mouth but arrested the motion.

"What do you mean?"

"You've got a crooked dealer."

The big man put the forkful of eggs back on the plate with a bang. Some of the egg jumped off the fork and onto the table.

"Who?"

"His name's Ed Brown."

Ordway stared at Clint for a long moment, then abruptly shouted, "Dillon!"

The bartender came out from behind the bar and approached the table.

"Yes, sir?"

"Mr. Adams tells me that Ed Brown has been cheating. Did you know that?"

"Not until he told me."

"When did he tell you?"

"Last night."

"And what did you think?"

"He said Brown was cheating for the house," Dillon said. "I didn't see nothin' wrong with that."

"There's no such thing as cheating for the house, Dillon," Ordway said. "All right, go back to the bar."

Dillon retreated and Ordway looked at Clint.

"What's he doing?"

"Dealing from the bottom."

"Stealing?"

"No," Clint said, "like I told Dillon, when a player has won a few games in a row, Brown stops him by dealing from the bottom."

"He's not stealing any money?"

"Not from you."

Ordway drummed his fingers on the table while he thought the situation over. Clint leaned over, poured himself another cup of coffee, then refilled Clark's cup after the gambler nodded.

"Okay," Ordway said, "I'll have to see for myself, you understand?"

"Of course I do," Clint said. He was still surprised that a crooked dealer had gotten past a man like John Ordway.

"I'll check him out tonight," Ordway said. "When do you want to question the others?"

"Today's good."

"Fine," Ordway said. "When you're ready we'll put you in one of the small rooms upstairs and I'll send them up one by one."

"That's good. Uh, Mr. Ordway—"

"Call me John," Ordway said.

"All right, John," Clint said. "Tell me, where do you live?"

"Upstairs," Ordway said. "I have the only living quarters on the premises."

"I'd like to see it."

Ordway closed his eyes.

"You're going to make me board up my windows, aren't you?"

THIRTEEN

Clint did, indeed, recommend to Ordway that he board up the windows of his living quarters until after the game was over. He told Ordway this as the three of them—Clint, Ordway and Dick Clark—came back down from the second floor.

"I can't make you do it," Clint said, "but if you don't, then that's a way in, and a potential problem."

"I have a carpenter coming to block off the back stairs," Ordway said. "I'll have him do my windows as well."

"Fine," Clint said. "I'll want to look at his work when he's finished."

"No problem."

Ordway had finished his breakfast, but sat down to have another cup of coffee.

"There's another thing," Clint said.

"What is it?" Ordway asked.

"Drinking during the game."

"Dick mentioned something about that," Ordway said. "I don't think we can stop a man from having a drink. If he gets drunk and pisses away his money that's better for everyone else in the game."

"And what if he gets so drunk that after he pisses away his money he decides to try to steal it back."

"Well, you'll excuse me for saying so, Clint," Ordway said, "but that would become your problem, then, wouldn't it?"

Clint had to admit Ordway had a point.

Later in the afternoon Clint was seated in one of the smaller rooms upstairs, interviewing the potential dealers for the game. Ordway had decided that they would not be able to use all his dealers, because he was going to keep his place open and operating downstairs while the big game was going on upstairs. Clint didn't approve of the decision, but he had already learned that those kinds of decisions were not going to be his, and he was gong to have to live with them or not take the job. Since he couldn't afford to play in the game, he knew the only way he could be a part of it was to work security, so he had to live with the decisions made by Ordway and—apparently, to a lesser extent—by Dick Clark.

He interviewed several of Ordway's dealers and about half a dozen others who had applied for the job. The interview consisted of some questions, and then watching the men handle a deck of cards. By the time he was ready to take a break, he had approved the four Ordway dealers, and two new ones.

When he came downstairs for a beer he saw that Clark was sitting at his private table, and Ordway was nowhere to be seen. He joined the gambler and asked Stacy to bring him a beer.

"How's it going up there?" Clark asked.

"Ordway's men look good," he said, "and I've picked two others, subject to your approval."

"If you picked them I'm sure they're okay."

"Won't Ordway want to see them?"

"If I okay them, it's fine with him."

So, in effect, Clint was picking the dealers. Interesting.

"What about the cheating dealer? Brown?"

"Ordway fired him."

"I thought he was going to watch him deal first?" Clint asked.

"He decided to take your word for it."

Stacy brought his beer, smiled at Clark and left.

"Seems like there's a lot of that going around," Clint said.

"What's that?"

"Taking my word for it."

"We're paying you a lot of money," Clark said. "We'd better be ready to take you at your word."

"Okay," Clint said. "I've got some more interviews this afternoon. By this evening I should have ten dealers and two relief dealers. Tomorrow I'll try for some extras in case we have more tables."

"That sounds good."

Clint looked around the room.

"Any players arrive?"

"Yes," Clark said, "they started drifting in this afternoon."

"Anybody I know?"

"Ben Thompson has a room at our hotel. In fact, he's got the room you should have had."

"Let him have it," Clint said. "I'm satisfied with what I've got. Anybody else?"

Clark reeled off a list of names, some of whom Clint knew, others he simply knew of, and some he'd never heard of.

"Where are they all going to stay?"

"There's a hotel in New Town, and several rooming houses on both sides of the line. Accommodations won't be a problem."

"That many people?"

"Ordway has made arrangements," Clark said. "We're erecting some tents around town for use, as well. Last ones in end up in the tents."

"I'm sure they won't mind the sleeping arrangements," Clint said, "as long as they get to play."

"I suppose."

"Anybody else I know of coming?"

"Luke, of course," Clark said, "and Bat. Brady, Bret, and some others."

"Sounds like a lot of diverse personalities," Clint said. "Should be interesting."

Clark stared into his beer mug.

"Dick?"

"Hmm?"

"What's on your mind?" Clint asked. "Is there something wrong?"

"Hmm?" Clark looked across the table at him. "Oh, no, I just have a lot on my mind. This is the largest game I've ever put together."

"I know," Clint said, "that's the reason I was surprised you chose to have it here."

"John insisted."

"And you gave in right away?"

"No," Clark said, "not right away . . . but eventually."

"And you're wondering if you made the right choice?"

"Yes . . . I've been having my doubts."

"About your choice of where to have the game," Clint asked, "or who your partner should be?"

Clark didn't answer. Clint finished his beer and stood up.

"I still have dealers to talk to," he said. "You've got some things to work out. If you want to talk later, or at any time—"

"I know," Clark said. "I'll keep that in mind. Thanks."

FOURTEEN

A man named Art Horne confused Clint. When he walked in he was wearing a gun with a well-worn handle, low on his hip, like he knew how to use it. If Clint had been hiring gunmen he would have expected them to look like Art Horne, who claimed to be a dealer.

"Where have you dealt before?" Clint asked as the man seated himself across the table from him. On the table was an open deck of cards and nothing else.

"All over." Horne was in his mid-thirties and his hands were free of calluses. He obviously did not have a history of hard work. Gunmen usually had hands like that, and gamblers.

"Like where?"

"Denver, Cripple Creek, Blackhawk, San Francisco—"

"Where in San Francisco?"

Horne pushed his hat back on his head.

"If you want written references it'll take me a few days," he said.

"I don't want anything in writing," Clint said. "Just a name will do."

"I've dealt for Duke Farrell in San Francisco."

63

"I know Duke," Clint said.

"Everybody knows Duke."

"I can check with him, you know."

"So check."

Now it was Clint's turn to sit back.

"You wear that gun as if you know how to use it."

"Is that what's botherin' you?" the man asked. "You of all people shouldn't be bothered by a man who knows how to use a gun."

"I'm not bothered," Clint said. "Fact is, I might have some use for a man who can use a gun."

"That would cost extra."

"Understood. Why don't you let me see what you can do with that deck of cards . . ."

When Clint was satisfied that Art Horne could handle the cards, he told him he was hired.

"You want to see me handle my gun?" the man asked.

"No," Clint said, "that's okay. We can get to that later, if the need arises."

Horne left and no one else came in. Eventually, Dick Clark came up.

"Looks like you're done for the day," he said. "How'd you do?"

"Ten and two, like I predicted," Clint said.

"That last fella looked more like a gunman."

"Yes," Clint said, "we discussed that. He can handle a deck of cards, though."

"Well, that's good. You want to get a steak?"

"Steak sounds good."

On the way downstairs Clint asked, "What about girls?"

"What about them?" Clark replied. "I like 'em. You like 'em, too."

"I like them a lot," Clint said, "but I was asking about using girls for the game. If Ordway's going to let the players drink, is he going to use the girls to serve?"

"I guess so."

"I should talk to each of the girls too, then."

"Even Stacy?" Clark asked.

"Stacy, Andy and . . . what's the redhead's name?"

"Trudy."

"Yeah, her, too?"

"Well, you can do that after dinner, then," Clark said, "although I don't see what you expect to find out."

"What if one of them has a boyfriend in the game?" Clint asked, as they left the saloon to go to the café. "And she looks at the cards when she's serving drinks? And somehow signals him? What if—"

"Okay, okay," Clark said. "I get the point."

"And if these girls are going to be serving at the game, who's going to be working downstairs?"

"You'll have to take that up with John," Clark said. "He's in charge of the girls."

"I'll talk to him about it," Clint said, when they reached old man O'Brien's café, "after dinner."

After another excellent steak dinner, Clint and Dick Clark went back to the saloon. Clark took Clint back to John Ordway's office and knocked on the door.

"Come!"

Clark opened the door and led Clint into the room.

"John, Clint has finished interviewing dealers for the day," the gambler said.

"There are just a few things to talk about," Clint said.

Ordway put down the pencil he'd been holding and sat back in his chair.

"Sure, have a seat."

"I'm, uh, gonna go out and have a drink," Clark said. "You two don't need me for this."

Before either Clint or John Ordway could say a word, Clark left the room.

"He's got something on his mind," Ordway said. "Has had for a while. I can't get it out of him."

"Neither can I," Clint said.

"Oh well," Ordway said with a shrug. "He's a grown man. He'll deal with it. What can I do for you, Clint?"

"Just a few things about the dealers . . ."

"Well," Ordway said, when Clint was done, "sounds like you've got everything in hand."

"On the dealers, yeah," Clint said. "I was wondering about the drinks."

"You're not going to argue with me about that, are you?" Ordway asked.

"No, nothing like that," Clint said. "I was just wondering if you were going to use your girls to serve the drinks, or hire some others."

"I'll hire some girls to work downstairs and use mine for the game," Ordway said. "That sound okay?"

"It sounds fine."

"That is," Ordway added, "unless you want to interview girls?"

"That won't be necessary," Clint said. "I'll just have a little talk with yours, though. So they know the rules."

Clint stood up.

"What rules are those?" Ordway asked.

"I don't know," Clint said, heading for the door. "I haven't thought them up, yet."

FIFTEEN

Clint talked with Trudy first, in the same room he'd used to interview the dealers.

"Mr. Ordway said you wanted to see me?" she asked, entering the room.

"Yes," he said, "we haven't met officially, Trudy. I'm Clint Adams."

She smiled and said, "Yes, I know who you are. Andy told me all about you."

"She did, huh?"

"Yes."

"Well . . . have a seat, Trudy. I need to ask you some questions."

Trudy was a tall, willowy redhead with an interesting sprinkle of freckles between her small breasts. She wore her dress very low to show them off. Tonight she had a green dress on, which showed off her emerald-green eyes to their best advantage.

"What's you last name?" he asked.

"O'Day," she said. "I'm Trudy O'Day."

Clint didn't know of any gamblers named O'Day.

"Have you been told that you and Andy and Stacy will

be serving drinks at this big poker game that's going to take place here?"

"Yes," she said, "Mr. Ordway told us."

"Do you know anyone who will be playing in the game?"

"Well," she said, "I know Mr. Clark. Will he be playing?"

"Not that I know of," Clint said, "unless he's changed his mind."

"And I know Mr. Ordway."

"He won't be playing."

She smiled flirtatiously and said, "And now I know you."

"I won't be playing, either."

She shrugged her pretty shoulders. "Then I guess I don't know anyone."

"No boyfriend or lover playing?"

"No, sir."

"And if someone walked in that you did know, would you tell me about it?"

"Would you want me to?"

"Yes."

"Then I would."

Clint stared at her for a few moments, and she stared right back without a hint of discomfort.

"All right, Trudy," he said. "I guess that's all. Would you send Stacy up?"

"Stacy?" she asked, standing. "Not Andy?"

"I'll be seeing Andy after Stacy," he said.

"I see," she said with a smirk. "You and Andy alone in this room for a while." She looked around. "Interesting."

Clint didn't respond and the redhead left the room. She

was very self-possessed and sure of herself. She could have been lying to him and he'd never know it. He decided to keep an eye on her.

On the other hand, Stacy Campbell was very nervous in his presence, and even more so when he started asking questions. He couldn't help but think that she was a total innocent.

"I don't understand," she said. "Have I done something wrong?"

"No, no," he said, "you haven't done anything wrong."

"Then why are you questioning me?" She was breathing so fast he thought she was going to pass out.

"You know what, Stacy? I don't have any more questions. You can go."

"I'm not fired?"

"No, you're not fired."

"I'm not in trouble?"

"No trouble," he said. "Just go downstairs and send Andy up."

"Okay," she said, turning to go. She stopped and turned back. "Is she in trouble?"

"No, Andy's not in any trouble," Clint said. "Everything's fine. Just send her up."

"What did you do to Stacy?" Andy asked.

"I didn't do anything to her."

"Yes, you did," she insisted, sitting opposite him. "You scared her to death."

"I just asked her some questions," he said. "The same questions I asked Trudy, and she was fine."

"Trudy's always fine," Andy said. "Nothing scares her."

"I wasn't trying to scare anyone," Clint said. "I'm in charge of security, I'm just questioning everyone who's going to work the game."

"So that's why I'm here?" she asked. "You want to know if I'm going to rob the game?"

"Are you?"

"If I could get away with it," she said, "I might. How about you?"

"No, I don't think I would," he said. "It's a lot of money, but I doubt I'd get to spend it."

"Well," she said, "what questions do you have for me?"

He asked her all the same questions he'd asked Trudy and Stacy, and got all the same answers. He had to admit to a certain prejudice when it came to Andy. He briefly considered rejecting her to serve drinks at the game, then thought that would just be silly. Questioning the waitresses was just a formality, anyway. If anyone was going to hold up the game it certainly wasn't going to be them.

"I guess we're finished here," he said.

"Is there anyone else who needs to come up and be questioned?" she asked.

"No, I'm done here."

"No," she said, "you're not."

"Andy—" he started, but stopped when she got up on the table, scooted across so that she was sitting in front of him, and abruptly pulled the top of her dress down so that her breasts spilled out in his face. It was something neither Stacy or Trudy could have done.

"Somebody might come in," he said, staring at her breasts.

"That just makes it exciting," she whispered.

"Andy—" he started, but she stopped him by grabbing his head and pulling his face into her breasts. It was so

fragrant there, and her nipples were as hard as little peb-
bles.

"Stop talking," she said, "or someone will come in and
catch us."

He pulled his face from her cleavage and said, "All
right, you want to play . . ."

He stood up, grabbed her ankles and tipped her over
backward onto the table. She gasped and reached out to
grab either edge of the table, as if she was afraid he was
going to toss her off, but that wasn't what he had in mind.

Not at all.

SIXTEEN

Clint grabbed the hem of Andy's dress and tossed it up above her waist. He tore something frilly from her and dropped it to the floor, then hurriedly undid his trousers before he burst from them.

"Hurry," she implored, "ooh, hurry . . ."

She was already wet and he slid right into her like one of them was greased. A moan escaped from her lips and she tried to wrap her legs around him, but he wouldn't let her. He grabbed ahold of her ankles, held her legs apart and began to fuck her so hard the table started moving across the room with every thrust. If business hadn't been booming downstairs he was sure they would have heard the table scraping along the floor.

"Jesus," she cried, "you're killing me. . . . don't stop . . ."

He had no intention of stopping. She wanted to play games but his only interest at the moment was to fuck her as fast and hard as he could, and find his own release. He reached up to fondle her breasts as he thrusted himself into her, then leaned over to kiss and bite her nipples. He had to let go of her ankles to do this and that's when she was able to wrap her legs around his waist. When he straightened up this time he slid his hands beneath her butt and she held on to the table so she wouldn't get pushed right off.

They were both grunting and groaning with every thrust and then suddenly his legs went weak at the same time she went rigid, her eyes opening wide.

"Oh God," she said, rushing over the edge, and a few rough thrusts later he followed her, and it was an amazing thing that the table didn't topple over, or simply collapse beneath them. . . .

Andy was on her feet, straightening her dress when the bartender, Ben Dillon, came in and eyed both of them suspiciously. To Clint the air smelled like pure sex, but he didn't know if the bartender could smell it where he was standing.

"What?" she demanded.

"Just wonderin' if you were gonna come back to work," he said. "It's real busy down there."

"Are we finished here, Mr. Adams?" she asked.

"I think I've got all the answers I needed from you," he replied.

"Well then," she said, looking at Dillon, "back to work."

She walked past the barman and went downstairs. Dillon didn't leave, though. He stood in the doorway looking at Clint.

"Is there something else?"

Dillon looked out in the hall, then pulled the door closed behind him. Clint studied the man, but didn't see where he might have had a weapon on him, so he just waited.

"You're picking people to work the game, right?"

"That's right."

"I'd like to work it."

"As what?"

"Bartender," Dillon said. "The girls will be serving drinks, right?"

"That's right."

"Well, they'll have to go up and down the stairs to get them," the man said, "unless you put a bar up here."

"Where?"

"One of the other rooms."

"The other rooms might be in use."

"Well, there's room in the hall, then, for a small bar."

"What about beer?"

"We can bring some kegs up here," Dillon said. "It can be done."

"But why?"

Dillon hesitated, then said, "This is the biggest game that's ever been held, right?"

"Well," Clint said, "outside of a major city, yes."

"I just want to be part of that."

Clint studied the man for a few moments, then said, "Have a seat."

"I can work it?"

"Let me ask you a few questions first," Clint said, "and then we'll see."

The bartender sat down, having no idea what had been happening on that table only moments before.

Clint asked Dillon many of the same questions he'd asked the dealers earlier in the day. He needed to know if anyone had any vested interest in who won the game. He prided himself on being able to tell when a man was lying and when he wasn't—most of the time, anyway. He didn't fool himself that he had the same ability when it came to women. No man did.

"So you don't care who wins or who loses?" Clint asked.

"Mr. Adams," Dillon said, "I don't even know who all is playin'. I just want to be up here while the game is goin' on."

"Well," Clint said, "if you can get your boss to agree, and replace you downstairs, I don't see why not."

"Thank you," Dillon said. "I'm sure I can get Mr. Ordway to agree."

"All right, then."

Dillon got up. "I can't tell you what this means to me."

"That's okay," Clint said. "Having a bar up here is a good idea. It will make it easier on the girls."

"Thanks again."

Dillon left and Clint found himself in need of a cold beer. He still couldn't believe what he and Andy had done on the table in between interviewing Stacy and Dillon. He'd practically split Andy in half and she had loved every minute of it.

Maybe he'd finally found a woman he wasn't going to be able to keep up with.

SEVENTEEN

It didn't really matter when the game was supposed to start, it would start when all the players were present. Ordway and Clark were not about to start the game without some of the big players.

Over the course of the next two days, most of the players drifted into town, and that included Ben Thompson and Bat Masterson. They were not the best of friends, but they had a healthy respect for each other. Luke Short arrived, and was friends with everyone—Thompson, Bat, Dick Clark, and Clint. He knew Ordway, but was not close friends with him. Bat and Luke were two of Clint's best friends.

Clint spent the better part of the two days sitting with Clark at his table, watching the players drift in. The main room upstairs had been all set up, and the back stairway had been walled off. They were waiting to see if they were going to have enough players to warrant using the other rooms.

When Ben Thompson walked in, Clint spotted him right away. He nodded to several of the players he obviously recognized and proceeded to the bar. He had a beer in his hand before he noticed Clint sitting in the back, and he raised the mug in greeting. Clint returned the gesture.

"You two friends?" Clark asked.

"Not really," Clint said. "We respect each other."

"Sounds like Thompson and Masterson."

"I don't think I have the same relationship with Ben that Bat has," Clint said. "There's something else going on there."

"Like what?"

"I don't think I ever want to know."

A couple of hours after Ben Thompson arrived Bat Masterson walked in. Clint had not seen Bat in some time and wasn't surprised at the pleasure he felt seeing Bat walk through the door. It was Bat who was probably his closest friend on earth, the man he would most like watching his back. Luke Short was a close second. And in a pinch, for a man to rely on and trust to be able to watch his back almost as well as those two, he'd pick Ben Thompson. Even Bat admitted that Thompson—with the possible exception of Clint Adams—was the best he'd ever seen with a pistol.

Bat approached the bar, saw Ben, exchanged a nod, and then collected a beer a little farther down the bar. This put him closer to Clint's table, and when he had beer in hand he walked over.

"Clint," he said, extending his hand. Clint stood and the two shared a warm handshake. Bat then looked at Dick Clark. "Good to see you, Dick."

"Bat." Clark stood and they shared a cordial handshake. "Have a seat," Clark invited.

Bat did, and looked at Clint.

"You playing in this shindig?"

Clint shook his head. "Security."

"Well," Bat said, "at least I know my money's safe."

"That's what we thought when we offered him the job," Dick Clark said.

Bat looked at Clark. "No, I meant I won't have to play against him. I'll have enough trouble with Thompson over there."

"And Luke," Clint said.

"That goes without sayin'," Bat said. "Is he here yet?"

"Haven't seen him," Clint said.

"Well," Bat said, looking around the room, "there's enough talent here for a game. I see Brady over there, and Charlie Cardiff, Sam Waterman and ol' Lucky Slim."

"Slim's here?" Clint asked, looking around.

"Table by the window, sittin' alone lookin' into a glass of whiskey," Bat said.

"Jesus," Clint said. "That's him? He's lost so much weight."

"Been sick, I hear," Bat said. "Same as Doc Holiday is what I heard. This might be his last game."

"How old is he?" Clark asked.

"Fifty."

"He looks seventy."

"I know," Bat said.

The three men sat there for a few moments looking across the floor at Alfred "Slim" Johnson, who had been called Lucky Slim for most of his life. Didn't seem like he was so lucky anymore.

Clint and Bat sat discussing what had gone on in each others lives since they had last seen each other. Dick Clark listened with great interest, because he knew he was sitting at a table with two legends—and Bat was twice a legend, both with a gun, and with a deck of cards.

Eventually, they got around to discussing the conditions of the game.

"Drinks during the game?" Bat asked. "Let's just hope Big Ed Cooley's not in the game."

"I know Ed Cooley," Clark said. "He's a decent card player."

"Bad drinker."

"I didn't know that about him."

"His wife left him a couple of years ago," Bat said. "He went right into a bottle and hasn't crawled out yet. When he gets mad and drunk he looks even bigger than six foot six."

"Speak of the devil," Clint said, and the other men looked over at the door, where a giant of a man had just entered—Ed Cooley.

"He looks drunk already. This may be your first duty as security," Bat said, "and the game hasn't even started yet."

"That depends," Clint said as Ed Cooley headed for the exact spot at the bar where Ben Thompson was standing, "on who he picks a fight with."

EIGHTEEN

Ed Cooley lurched to the bar. Clint hated drunks and guns, and it was worse when the drunk was a big man who knew how to use a gun. If Cooley picked on Thompson though, Ben would shoot him down. There's no way Ben Thompson would try to fight with the man.

Clint looked at Clark.

"Bat's right," the man said. "The game hasn't even started yet. This isn't your job."

"Who's is it?"

Clark shrugged. "Maybe Dillon."

"The bartender?" Clint asked. "There's no way he can handle Ben and Cooley. Ordway doesn't have anyone working here to handle this kind of situation?"

"Dillon's got a shotgun behind the bar," Clark said. "If he takes it out now—"

"—Somebody'll get killed," Clint said, and left the table.

Bat looked at Clark. "What're you gonna do?" he asked, and followed Clint.

Cooley had already nudged Thompson with his big shoulder by the time Clint and Bat reached the bar.

"Watch what you're doin'!" Thompson snapped.

"Ben!" Bat said, coming up on the other side of Thompson. "Let me buy you a drink."

"Wha—Masterson?"

On the other side of him, Clint got between Cooley and Thompson and said, "Come on, Ed."

"I ain't had a drink yet," the big man bellowed.

"Let's go down to the other end of the bar and I'll buy you one," Clint promised.

"You will? Hey, you're awright. Who are you?"

"I'm your friend, right now," Clint said, hustling Cooley away from Ben Thompson, while Bat convinced Ben he really wanted to buy him a drink. . . .

Later, after Clint had convinced Ed Cooley to go to his hotel and sleep it off, he and Bat returned to Dick Clark's table.

"That was nicely done," Clark said. "Not a shot fired."

"It wasn't easy," Clint said. "Moving Ed Cooley is like trying to move a mountain."

"Oh, poor you," Bat said. "I'm the one who had to have a drink with Ben Thompson. He couldn't believe I was buying."

"Where's Ordway?" Clint asked. "Doesn't he ever come out of his office to see how business is?"

"The saloon is not his business, Clint," Clark said. "The game is."

"He's cutting the pots?" Bat asked.

"Yes."

"I hate that."

"That's how he'll make his money," Clark said.

"Why doesn't he just play for it, like everyone else?"

"He's not a gambler," Clark said.

"I heard that about him," Bat said. "Never plays?"

"Never does, never has."

"There's enough money in this game," Clint said.

"I'm here," Bat said, "I'm not gonna turn around and leave—but I really do hate that."

"Let me buy you a beer to soothe you," Clint said.

"Good," Bat said, "it'll make up for the one I had to buy Thompson."

"Relax, both of you," Clark said. "I'll buy you each one and then I'm turning in. We've got a big day tomorrow. With any luck, we'll start the game tomorrow night."

"The sooner the better, for me," Bat said. "What is it with this town, anyway? Seems to have an identity crisis of some kind."

"You don't know the half of it," Clint said.

NINETEEN

After Clark turned in, Clint and Bat remained at the table. Clint was surprised when the door to John Ordway's office opened and the man stepped out. He saw them and approached the table.

"Mind if I join you gents?"

"Have a seat," Clint said. "It's your place."

Ordway sat and reached his hand across the table to Bat.

"We know each other, don't we, Bat?"

"We've crossed paths once or twice," Bat admitted, shaking the man's hand.

"I'm glad you decided to play in this game."

"I might not have, if I'd known you were raking the pots."

"I've got to make my money any way I can, Bat," Ordway said. "I don't have the talent, or—frankly the nerve—to sit down with you at a poker table."

"Somehow I doubt that," Bat said. "I think there's another reason you don't play."

"And what would that be?"

"I don't know," Bat said. "I'm just saying you don't seem like a man with no nerve."

"What about talent?"

"Everybody's got a talent for something," Clint said.

"Mine is for making money," John Ordway announced. "It's just not for gambling."

"You don't call what you do gambling?" Bat asked.

"There are no sure things in gambling, isn't that right?" Ordway asked.

"Yes," Bat said.

Ordway spread his hands. "It's a sure thing that I will make money from this poker game, therefore I'm not gambling."

"But investing money in opening this place," Clint said, "here, in a town like Big Fork . . . wouldn't you call that a gamble?"

"I have a knack for knowing where businesses will make money," Ordway said. "I just don't see it as a gamble."

"Well," Bat said, looking at Clint, "if you're that good at what you do, maybe it isn't gambling."

Clint shrugged, and then his eye was caught by someone entering the saloon.

"Speaking of gamblers," he said, and everyone followed his eyes.

"One of the best," Bat said, and waved his hand at Luke Short, who bypassed the bar and came right over to the table.

"Hello, gents," Luke said, shaking hands with all three and joining them.

Ordway waved a hand and Trudy appeared at the table.

"Beer all around?" he asked the table, and they all nodded.

"I need one," Luke said. "Been travelin' most of the

day to get here. Not an easy place to reach."

"By design," Ordway said.

"I saw John McNee when I was checking into my hotel," Luke said. "Thank you for the fine room, by the way." McNee was a top poker player from England. Clint had seen him play.

"I put all the top players in the same hotel," Ordway said. "Sort of my way of predicting who will be playing at the final table."

"How many tables will there be?" Luke asked.

"We'll find out in the morning when players begin to register for the game," Ordway said.

"And when will we start?" Bat asked.

"Probably the next day," Ordway said, "Monday. We could start Sunday but the good people of Big Fork are already convinced that I'm the devil."

"That's okay," Bat said. "I always like a day to get acclimated to a new town."

"And altitude," Luke added.

Trudy returned with the beers and Clint noticed there were only three. As she set them down, Ordway stood up.

"I have work to do, gents. Welcome to all of you, and good luck when the game starts."

"Who's your money on, John?" Luke asked. "If you were a gambler, I mean."

"If I was a gambler, Luke," Ordway said, "my money would always be on you." He looked at Clint and Bat. "No offense."

"None taken," they both said.

Ordway walked off, and the three men picked up their beers.

"Nice lookin' girl," Bat said, looking at Trudy.

"A little jumpy," Clint said. "And I think she's got something with Dick Clark."

"Where is Dick?" Luke asked.

"He turned in a while ago," Clint said.

"That's what I'm thinking of doing," Bat said. "I'm feelin' the same kind of aches you are, my friend." He spoke to Luke.

"What's the rest of this town like?" Luke asked Clint.

"You wouldn't believe it," Clint said, "but I have found a good place to eat."

"Dinner or breakfast?" Bat asked.

"Both," Clint said. "I'll take you both there in the morning."

"That's it, then," Bat said. He pushed away the remainder of his beer. "I'm off to bed."

"I'll walk with you," Luke said.

"I'll make it three," Clint said. "I want to be here early to see who's here for the game."

"Any poker player worth his salt, I'd say," Bat said.

"I hope so," Luke said. "I'm looking forward to takin' everyone's money."

"Everyone?" Bat asked.

"Yes," Luke said, 'that includes you. . . ."

Clint listened to his two best friends bicker good-naturedly all the way back to the hotel.

TWENTY

Outside the saloon, two men watched the trio walk across the street to the hotel.

"It's not going to be easy with those three around," one man said.

"Two of them are playing," the second man said. "They'll be distracted."

"So that only leaves the Gunsmith to deal with," the first man said. "That supposed to make me feel better?"

"He's just one man."

Joe Best stared at his partner, Hank Dennis. He could barely see him in the light cast by the half moon.

"He's the Gunsmith," Best said.

"The boss has this figured, Joe," Dennis said. "Besides, it's not gonna be just you and me."

"Better not be," Best said. "Any idea how many more men he's gonna use?"

"No," Dennis said. "All I know is we're the first two."

"Why us?"

"I've worked for him before."

"But he's gonna need better guns than ours."

"He'll get them," Hank said, "if he doesn't already have them."

The three men went into the hotel lobby.

"What do we do now?" Best asked.

"We get a drink," Dennis said, "or two."

"We're done watchin'?"

"We're done watchin'," Dennis said, "for tonight."

The man planning to rob the game knew that doing so would make him a legend. Especially considering how many legends there would be participating in the game. And to top it all off, the Gunsmith being not only in charge of security, but all the security there was. When word got out about what he did, he'd be the biggest legend of all, and he could stop living in the shadows of others.

He knew that Best and Dennis were idiots, but they'd serve their purpose. He had real guns coming in for the real action, and they were also eager to enhance their reputations at the cost of Bat Masterson, Luke Short, Ben Thompson and Clint Adams.

Personally, he thought they were all crazy to try it—especially him—but that was the fun.

Wasn't it?

TWENTY-ONE

Clint hadn't noticed that Andy had left the saloon before he did, but he did notice that she was in his bed when he entered the room.

"How'd you get in here?" he asked.

She shifted under the sheet and said, "Are you mad at me?"

"No," he said, "I was just wondering."

She stretched and he could see the outline of her nipples beneath the sheet.

"I just smiled at the desk clerk and he let me in," she said. "I want some more of what you gave me on that table today."

"To get more of that," Clint said, "we'd have to do it someplace where we could get caught."

"Well," she said, getting to her knees, "I didn't mean exactly that. I just meant . . ." She let the sheet dropped away from her so he could see her opulent curves in all their glory. Her skin was flawless and the tangle of hair between her legs a black forest.

He removed his clothing slowly while she watched, finishing by hanging his gun belt on the bedpost.

"You think you're gonna need that?" she asked.

He got into bed with her, gathered her into his arms and said, "A man never knows."

He woke the next morning with her firm backside pressed against his groin, his erection already crawling up her butt. He reached around with one hand to cup one of her full breasts and the other he slid down into her tangle of hair. He slid his middle finger up and down until she was moist and ready, then slid his penis up in between her thighs and into her.

"Ooh," she said, moving her legs to better accommodate him, "what a nice way to wake up."

"The best," he said into her ear.

She began to push her butt back against him each time he thrusted himself into her, and then she rolled over so she was on her stomach. He supported himself with a hand on either side of her and began to move in and out of her eagerly. She was so excited he swore his cock was longer and harder than it had ever been. With every moan and cry that escaped from her lips he became even more excited.

He pushed himself up onto his knees and brought her butt off the bed so he could grab her on each side. Holding her hips that way he drove himself into her even harder until with a loud roar he emptied himself into her.

They spooned for half an hour until they each caught their breath and then he said, "Got to go. I promised two friends I'd buy them breakfast."

"Do you mind if I stay here a while?" she asked. "You tired me out."

"I tired you out?" he asked, laughing. He sat up, swung

his feet to the floor, then reached back and slapped her naked butt. "You stay as long as you like. I'll see you later at the saloon."

She rolled over on her stomach and he stared briefly at the line of her back as it disappeared between the chunky cheeks of her ass, then forced himself to get up, get dressed and get out.

When he got to the lobby, Bat and Luke were already there waiting for him.

"We thought you were gonna sleep in," Bat complained.

"I wasn't sleeping," Clint said.

"See, I told you," Luke said, nudging Bat. "That's our boy."

They had agreed to meet in the lobby at 8 A.M.

"I'm only ten minutes late," he said, "and you can't believe how strong I had to be to come down here."

"Maybe we should go up and take a look?" Bat asked.

"I don't think the lady would like that," Clint said.

"The redhead?" Bat asked.

"No, the blonde," Luke said.

"Wrong on both counts," Clint said. "Let's go and eat."

Old man O'Brien welcomed Clint and shook hands with Bat and Luke after being introduced.

"I'm honored to have such distinguished guests," he said. "Steak and eggs for everyone? You won't believe how good it will be."

"I'll believe it," Clint said. "I had it already."

They all agreed to steak and eggs.

"Why aren't you playing in this game?" Luke asked Clint. "There's a lot of money at stake."

"And somebody has to make sure it's safe," Clint said.

"If it's money I'll back you," Luke said. "I'd be hedging my bet, that way."

"I could go for half of that," Bat said.

"It's a generous offer on both your parts, but I really don't want to play against the two of you. You're too good."

"And you're a big liar." Bat said, "but let us know if you change your mind."

"There should be lots of backers here," Luke said. "I heard Harry the Bank is coming."

"The Bank will bankroll more than one player," Bat said. "You could be one of them, Clint."

"We'll see," Clint said. "You fellas just want to take my money."

"Hell," Bat said, "we want to take everybody's money!"

O'Brien's steak and eggs impressed Bat and Luke, and impressed Clint a second time.

"Even the coffee's good," Luke said. "This place is almost reason enough to move here."

"Wait until you taste his pie," Clint said.

"Will you be taking all your meals here?" Bat asked.

"Probably."

"What about the other part of town?" Luke asked. "They call it New Town?"

"Not much different from here, if you ask me," Clint said. "But take a look, if you like. I have to get over to the saloon."

"So do we," Bat said. "We've got to secure our chairs at the game and see who else has put in an appearance."

Clint paid the bill and they walked back to the saloon together. The front doors were open and on the inside it looked like they were doing a brisk business, except no one was drinking.

"Looks like we have to stand in line," Bat said.

Clint looked around and spotted Dick Clark.

"Maybe not," he said. "Wait here."

Clint went over and joined Clark, who had his ear cocked toward a man who was talking to him.

"No," he told the man, "they have to have the ten thousand on them now."

"Okay," the other man said, and left.

"Good morning," Clark said. "It's a madhouse."

"I can see that," Clint said. "Bat and Luke are here. Do they have to stand in line?"

"Not down here," Clark said. "Take them upstairs. That's where most of the name players are. Thompson's up there already, and McNee and some of the others."

"Okay," Clint said. "I'll tell them."

He started back toward Bat and Luke, was jostled on both sides and thought this was a bad situation for men like them. Anybody in this crowd could take a shot at one of them. Upstairs would definitely be better for the three of them.

He was almost back to Bat and Luke when somebody grabbed his left arm.

"Adams!"

He turned quickly to find himself facing Harry Palmer—Harry the Bank.

"Harry," he said, "don't grab me like that in this kind of a crowd."

"Sorry," the dapper little man said. "I heard you weren't playing in this game. I'm willin' to back you."

"That's okay, Harry," Clint said. "I'm not playing by choice."

"I seen you play, Adams," Palmer said. "You're good enough to win this. I'll put up the entry fee for twenty-five percent of the pot."

"How many players have you made that same deal with?" Clint asked.

"None as good as you."

"Well, I hope you've got a good one, Harry, because I'm not playing. Excuse me."

"Let me know if you change your mind."

Harry the Bank went off in search of another player for his stable, and Clint grabbed Bat and Luke.

"Go upstairs," he said. "Apparently, that's where the elite are."

"What about you?" Luke asked.

"I think most of the money is down here," Clint said. "I better start doing my job."

"Okay," Bat said, "we'll see you later."

As Bat Masterson and Luke Short made their way to the stairs, Clint moved back through the crowd to find Dick Clark again.

"Who's collecting the money?" he asked.

"Come with me," Clark said.

"Are you armed?"

Clark held open his jacket so Clint could see the gun beneath his arm.

"Okay," Clint said, "take me to the money."

TWENTY-TWO

The entry fee money was put into a cash box, and would later be transferred to a Mosler safe that was upstairs in the main room. This was Clint's suggestion. That way, the money was right there in the room with the players, and Clint could watch them all. Ordway agreed and had the safe moved into the room.

Ben Dillon was seated at a table accepting the money, while Dick Clark stood to one side of him and Clint stood on the other. Most of the players were strangers to Clint, who was familiar with the regular members of the fraternity of gamblers. It seemed as if players were coming out of nowhere to play in this game. He would have liked to have been upstairs to see who was signing up there. There was no money being exchanged there, though. Ordway and Clark had made other arrangements in order to collect money from the likes of Bat Masterson, Ben Thompson and Luke Short.

It took about three hours for the line to dwindle down, and by the time they were done—with Ordway checking upstairs—they had a hundred and sixteen players signed up to play. At ten thousand dollars each that was a million, one hundred sixty thousand that would be going into that safe.

Someone was going to leave Big Fork, Montana a millionaire.

Clint, Dick Clark and John Ordway went upstairs, with Clint carrying the cash box from the bartender. Ordway told Dillon to start serving drinks to the participants, who had spread out and were seated at tables.

On the second floor, Clint found the cream of the gamblers. There were about twenty of the top players in the country and—with John McNee from England and a man called Canadian Jack Dean—outside the country.

Clint and Clark stood between the group and John Ordway as he opened the safe and deposited the money inside. He then stood and looked at Dick Clark.

"Dick, we've filled the game and all the major players who said they would attend are here," he said. "I think we should start the game up tonight."

"On Sunday?" Clint asked. "Aren't you afraid the town will hang you?"

"We'll start one minute after midnight," Clark said.

"That sounds good to me," Ordway said. "I'll go downstairs and announce the starting time. You fellas can spread the word up here."

"Fine," Clark said.

Ordway left the room but before Clark could make any kind of announcement Clint grabbed his arm.

"What's wrong?"

"I need one more man."

"For what?"

"There's over a million dollars in this safe, Dick," Clint said. "I can't stay here, or stay awake, twenty-four hours to guard it. I'll be here while the game is being played, but what about today, between now and then?"

"Who can you trust?"

"I talked to a fella who wanted to deal, and I had a good feeling about him," Clint said. "I think I'll try and get him to stand guard rather than dealing."

"Can you trust him?"

"Well," Clint said, "I don't think he can get into that safe alone, so unless he came here with help, intending to break into a Mosler, I'd be inclined to trust him . . . a bit."

"Okay," Clark said. "You get him if you can."

"You'll pay him?"

"Sure."

"More than he would have got dealing?"

"Yeah, why not?" Clark said. "We don't pay the dealers that much, anyway."

"That's a good way to look at it," Clint said, and they went to make the announcement of the game's starting time.

TWENTY-THREE

Clint found Art Horne and took him to a small saloon located in New Town.

"Why are we drinking here and not at Mr. Ordway's saloon?" Horne asked.

"I wanted to talk to you away from all the activity," Clint said.

Horne looked around. They were seated at a table, and except for the bartender, they were the only ones in the place.

"Well, this is about as far from the activity as we could get," Horne said. "What's on your mind?"

"I told you I might want to press you into service for the purposes of security."

"Yeah, but—"

"Well, that's what I'm doing," Clint said. "I want you to forget about dealing and just work security with me."

"But . . . why? What's changed?"

Clint explained about the safe and the fact that they needed someone to stand guard when Clint wasn't available.

"And why wouldn't you be available?"

"Because I have to sleep sometime," Clint said.

"Nobody thought of this beforehand?"

"As a matter of fact," Clint said, "no."

"Why would they hire you to stand security all by yourself when it's not a one-man job?"

"That's a good question," Clint said, "but I'll deal with that later. For now let me know if you'll do it."

"For the same money?" Horne asked. "If it's the same money, to tell you the truth, I'd rather deal."

"No, it's more money," Clint said.

"Because to tell you the truth," Horne went on, "I think this game is gonna be hit."

"Why do you say that?" Clint asked. "Have you heard something?"

"Yes," Horne said, "I've heard there's a lot of money in this game. How could somebody *not* try to hit it?"

"Maybe the people who are in the game will scare them away," Clint said. "Bat Masterson? Ben Thompson?"

"Clint Adams?"

"Maybe."

"I don't think so," Horne said. "There's just too much damn money in one place."

"So if you think there's a danger of it being hit, why do you want to be part of it?"

"Because, one way or another, this game is gonna make history," Horne said. "Who wouldn't want to be part of that?"

"So how do you want to be part of it?" Clint asked. "As a dealer, or working security with me?"

"Working security at this game with the Gunsmith," Horne said. "I really can't pass that up, can I?"

"I don't know, can you?"

"No, I can't," Horne said, "but for more money, right?"

"Right."

Horne finished his beer and set it down.

"So, do you want to see me shoot?"

"No," Clint said, "I won't need to. Just let me see your gun."

"My gun?"

Clint nodded, put out his hand. Horne hesitated, then took his gun from his holster and gave it to him. It was a .45 Peacemaker, well-oiled and cared for. Clint checked the action, and the loads, then handed it back.

"Nice weapon, well-cared for," he said, as Horne eased it back into his holster. "Do you take care of your rifle as well?"

"And my saddle," Horne said. "You want to see them, too?"

"No, that won't be necessary," Clint said. "You'll do." He stood up.

"Let's go over to the saloon and I'll show you what I want you to do."

TWENTY-FOUR

"The money's in here?" Horne asked, putting his hand on the four-foot-high safe.

"Yep."

Horne rubbed his hand over the hard metal surface of the top of the safe.

"How much?"

"Over a million."

Horne raised his eyebrows.

"Tempted?"

"Let's just say," Horne replied, "that if the door was ajar I might be tempted."

Clint stared at the door of the safe and wondered if he would have been tempted, also?

"So what's my job?" Horne asked.

"Keep people away from the safe while this room is empty," Clint said.

"And how often will it be empty?"

"From now until midnight, and perhaps when there's a break in the game."

"How long will there be breaks in the game for?"

"Not long," Clint said. "Maybe an hour."

"They won't break for sleep?"

"No," Clint said. "The game will go on."

"What about sleep?"

Clint shrugged. "Anybody falls asleep, they lose."

Art Horne looked around the room at the ten empty tables and a hundred empty chairs. They had all been brought in since Clint had last seen the room.

"No windows."

"By design," Clint told him.

"Any other rooms?"

"One, or maybe two," Clint said. "I'm not really sure. Why don't we check?"

They left the main room and walked to the other two. One had ten tables set up, the other six.

"Three rooms," Horne said, "two of us."

"The third room won't last long," Clint said. "Enough players will bust out of the game in the first few hours to eliminate it. But you won't have to worry about that." He looked at Horne. "Your only concern will be that first room and the safe."

Horne looked around and nodded.

"You gonna sit out in the hall?"

Clint nodded.

"As long as there's one room."

"You'll miss the game."

"Just the beginning," Clint said. "Once it gets down to one room, I'll be able to watch."

They walked back to the main room.

"When do I start?"

"Get something to eat and come back," Clint said.

"No," Horne said, "I can start now. You can send something up for me to eat later."

"I'll bring it myself," Clint said.

"Suit yourself."

Horne walked to one of the tables, commandeered a chair, brought it back, put it in front of the safe and sat down.

"I'm on the job."

"I'll get you part of your pay up-front," Clint said. "I'll bring it when I bring the food. Steak okay?"

Horne thought about it, then said, "Beef stew, I think. Plenty of biscuits."

Clint was sure O'Brien would be able to do a great beef stew.

"Uh, the food is included, isn't it?" Horne asked.

"Yep," Clint said, "food is included."

TWENTY-FIVE

On the way in, Clint had spotted both Bat and Luke in the saloon, which was now apparently open for business. As he looked around, on the way down the stairs, he saw his two friends seated at a table together, and Bat waved him over. He saw a few of the other gamblers scattered around, but not enough to fill the place up.

He stopped at the bar for a beer before joining Bat and Luke.

"Ordway decided to open for business?" Clint asked. "On Sunday?"

"We're not really open," Dillon said. "We're serving drinks to the gamblers."

Clint looked around as Dillon placed a beer in front of him.

"I see some men here who aren't in the game."

Dillon shrugged and said, "If they come in and they want a drink . . ."

"I see," Clint said. "Thanks."

He went over to the table and sat down with Bat and Luke.

"What's going on?" Bat asked.

Clint told them about putting Art Horne upstairs to watch the safe. When Luke asked him who Horne was Clint explained how he had met the man.

"You figure you know him well enough to have him watch over a million dollars?" Bat asked.

"I don't think he's going to make off with the safe, if that's what you mean."

"He could blow it," Luke said. "It's been known to happen."

"I guess he could, but he didn't have any dynamite on him when I left him."

"Well," Bat said, "I think it's smart of you to add a man. Did you see the setup?"

"Three rooms," Clint said, "six tables in the smaller room."

"We'll whittle that down in the first few hours," Luke said.

"I figured that."

"Down to one room in no time," Bat said.

"The game won't really start until we're down to three or four tables," Luke said.

"And then it'll really get going," Bat said, "when we're down to one."

"You fellas figure to be on the last table, huh?"

They both looked at him like he was crazy.

"We wouldn't be here if we didn't figure that."

"Okay, wise guys," Clint said, "tell me who's going to be on the last table with you?"

"We're starting with eight to a table," Luke said, "so by the time we get down to the last eight, there'll be me and Bat, Ben Thompson—"

"Really?" Bat asked, interrupting him. "You think Thompson's that good?"

"Don't let you personal feelings get in the way, Bat," Luke said. "He's that good."

"Well, okay," Bat said. "I think McNee will be there."

"Really?" Luke asked. "The British fella?"

"You just don't like him because he's dressed better than you," Bat said. "Don't let your personal feelings get in the way."

"Okay," Luke said, "what about Canadian Jack?"

"And Lucky," Bat said. "He's on his last game, probably. At least, from what I hear."

"Brady and Bret should be there," Luke said.

"Not that guy," Bat said with a face.

"Which one?"

Before the two men could go any further Clint asked, "Either of you plan on getting any sleep before the game?"

Bat looked around. "That looks like what most of them are doin', doesn't it?"

"Yeah," Luke said, "I'm not as young as I used to be. I'll have to get some sleep."

"Ravages of time," Bat said.

Clint finished his beer and said, "I've got some things to see to. See you both later."

"You gonna eat at that same place?" Luke asked.

"Most likely."

"Maybe we'll see you there," Bat said.

Clint nodded and left the saloon.

Across the street both Joe Best and Hank Dennis watched him leave.

"That money's up there," Best said.

"So?"

"We could go and get it," Best said, "just the two of us."

"And how you gonna get the safe open?" Dennis asked.

Best shrugged and said, "It's been done."

"Yeah," Dennis said, "with explosives. You got any?"

"No."

"Then keep yer stupid ideas to yerself," Dennis said. "We're just gonna do what we're told and take our cut, like everybody else. There's plenty to go around."

"Yeah, but there's—"

"Joe."

"Yeah?"

"Shut up before I shoot you."

TWENTY-SIX

Clint went to the livery stable to make sure that Eclipse was being well cared for. Once the game started he didn't know if he'd have the time. He found that the livery man was being true to his word. The big Darley Arabian was in fine shape.

Next, he went to his room to check and make sure his rifle was in working order. He'd have it with him when he was standing guard in the hall outside the poker rooms. Clint also loaded the little New Line Colt. He decided if he was going to guard over a million dollars he'd better be well-armed. He unbuttoned his shirt and tucked the gun against his belly.

That done, he decided to check the perimeter of the hotel to make sure there was no way in he didn't know about. After that he planned on seeing both Clark and Ordway for some last-minute business.

Dick Clark looked out the window of his hotel and watched as Clint Adams crossed the street toward him. When Clint disappeared from view, Clark assumed he had entered the saloon. He turned away from the window and looked at Stacy, as the blonde reclined on his bed asleep. Her body was long and sleek, her skin flawless, her breasts delightfully small but firm. He was glad she had been bold enough to bring them together, because he didn't know if he would have done it. Certainly once the game got underway he probably would not have.

He wondered about the game, and about his partnership with John Ordway. Was it something he was going to come to regret?

Or was it something he already regretted?

John Ordway sat in his office, and his heart was beating fast. In a matter of hours the game would be underway. If everything went right, he would come out of this with a lot of money. Once he had it he'd sell this place and move on, set up another big game someplace else, only next time he wouldn't need Dick Clark, or anyone else as a partner. He should be able to go back to doing business the way he used to, before some reversals of fortune had put him in this position.

Denver, he thought, or maybe San Francisco.

Clint walked once around the saloon, checking doors and windows, backing up so he could see the second floor. It didn't really matter if someone could get in downstairs, they were still going to have to get past him to get upstairs.

Idly, he wondered which of his friends, Bat or Luke, was going to walk away from this game a millionaire. Or would someone else be able to beat both of them? He really would have liked to be part of the game, but he didn't kid himself that he was in the same class with players like Bat Masterson and Luke Short. Or even Ben Thompson.

When he reentered the saloon both Bat and Luke had gone, as had most of the other players. The few men who were standing at the bar, or sitting down, looked like miners or townsmen.

He went to the bar and asked Dillon, "Have you seen Clark?"

"I think he's in his room."

"And Ordway?"

"His office, probably."

Clint nodded, turned and walked to Ordway's door. When he knocked he heard the man call, "Come."

"Clint," Ordway said, "I'm glad you're here. I was about to have a brandy to celebrate the start of the game. Join me?"

Clint would have preferred beer, but he said, "Why not?"

He took the glass the man handed him and they both seated themselves across the desk from each other.

"Here's to a successful game," Ordway said, raising his glass.

"I have a question for you."

"What's that?" Ordway asked, putting his glass down.

"Who's handling the side action?"

Ordway hesitated, then said, "What side action?"

"Come on, John," Clint said. "A game like this? Somebody's taking side action, and being the smart man you are, you're bound to have a piece of it."

Ordway picked up his glass, drained it and set it down again. Clint realized he was using the time to think.

"Come on, John," he said. "You hired me to overlook security. I've got to know everybody who's involved with this game."

"Jim Canaday's handling the side action."

"Canaday?" Clint frowned. "Where is he? I haven't see him."

"I've got him in a hotel in New Town."

"Why haven't I heard that he's taking side bets?"

"Are you going to make a bet?"

"No."

"That's why you haven't heard."

"And you're getting a piece of his action?"

"No."

"John—"

"He's getting a piece of my action."

"So when you say you don't gamble, you're not exactly telling the truth, are you?"

Ordway sighed and said, "I suppose not, if you look at that as gambling."

"I do." Clint put his glass down on Ordway's desk, virtually untouched, and stood up.

"What hotel?" Clint asked.

"Why?"

"I want to talk to him."

"What for?"

"To find out who he's talked to," Clint said. "I don't know how much you know about Canaday, but if he sees an opening to make a buck he'll take it—and there are over a million of them to make on this game."

"You think Canaday would plan to rob the game?"

"I don't think he'll plan it," Clint said. "He's not that smart. I do think he'd open his mouth about it to someone. I want to find out who he's been talking to."

Ordway thought it over a moment, then said, "He's at the Hotel Grand."

"I'll go and talk to him now," Clint said. "I've got a man named Art Horne watching the safe. If you go up there, make sure he knows who you are. He has orders to shoot anyone who goes near it."

Clint started for the door, then stopped and turned around.

"Why would you pick Canaday to handle the book on the game?" he asked.

"You assumed the action was his," Ordway said. "Anybody else would have demanded the same. With Canaday, the action is mine, and he gets a cut." Ordway spread his hands. "It's just business, not really gambling."

"Yeah," Clint said. "Keep telling yourself that."

TWENTY-SEVEN

The Hotel Grand wasn't so grand, but it was bigger than any other hotel in town—Old Town or New Town. Ordway hadn't told Clint what room Canaday was in, but that didn't matter. The man seemed to have set up shop in the hotel saloon.

When Clint entered there were three men standing in front of a table that Canaday was seated at. While Clint watched, Canaday touched a lead pencil to his tongue and made a notation, and then the men turned and left. Clint took the opportunity to approach the table.

"What are the odds on Bat Masterson?" he asked.

"Ah, now you're talkin' about one of the favorites," Canaday said, before looking up. "I tell you what., I'll give you—" He stopped short when he did look up.

"Clint!" he said.

"Hello, Jim."

"W-what are you doin' here?"

"I'm handling security for the game."

"I heard that," Canaday said, "but . . . are you lookin' ta make a bet?"

"Not with you."

"Uh, then what can I do for you?"

Clint sat down opposite the man. Canaday was wearing a black suit that was about ten years old, with frayed collar and cuffs. His shirt was more gray than the original white. Clint wondered why Ordway would bring Canaday into the mix.

"Jim," Clint said, "this game is way beyond anything you've ever dealt with before."

Canaday leaned back in his chair and said, "I can handle it."

"Are you sure?"

The man hesitated, then said, "Mr. Ordway must think so, or he wouldn't have hired me."

"Here's what I want to know," Clint said, leaning his elbows on the table. "Who did you tell about this?"

"Me?" Canaday could not lean back far enough in his chair, no matter how hard he tried. Clint almost expected the back of the chair to snap off. "I didn't tell nobody."

Clint stared at him.

"Who would I tell?"

"I don't know, Jim," Clint said. "That's what I'm trying to find out right now."

Canaday steeled himself and stopped trying to put more space between himself and Clint.

"Look Adams," he said, "I know this is a big deal for everybody. It's a huge deal for me, and I'm not gonna mess it up."

"So you didn't tell anybody about this big deal of yours?" Clint demanded.

Canaday swallowed and said, "Well, maybe I told one or two friends . . ."

Now it was Clint's turn to sit back in his chair.

"Who did you tell?"

"Just a couple of guys . . ."

"And you don't expect them to tell anyone else?" Clint asked. "Like maybe somebody who'd want to come and rob the game?"

"Now why would they want to do that?" Canaday asked.

"Maybe because there's over a million dollars involved?" Clint asked. "Not to mention whatever bets you're taking."

Canaday looked worried.

"You really think somebody will try to hit this game?" he asked.

"I don't know," Clint said. "It depends on who you told about it, and who they told." Clint stood up and pointed a finger at the other man. "Don't talk to anyone else about this game, Canaday."

"I won't."

"I mean it."

"I know," Canaday said. "Don't worry, Adams. I ain't stupid."

"Not when it comes to adding and subtracting, maybe," Clint said. "Just keep it in mind that I wouldn't take it kindly if you talked to anyone else."

"I got it," Canaday mumbled.

Clint gave the man one last stare and then left the saloon.

Joe Best and Hank Dennis watched as Clint left the small saloon, and then entered. They walked directly to Jim Canaday's table.

"What can I do—" Canaday said, then stopped when he saw who it was. "Jesus! What are you two doin' here?"

"We saw Adams leave," Dennis said. "What did he want?"

"He wanted to know who I been talkin' to," Canaday

said, "and I don't want him to see me talkin' to you guys."

"What did you tell him?"

"Nothin'."

"Are you sure?" Joe Best asked. "We wouldn't take it kindly if you mentioned our names to him."

"Why would I do that?" Canaday asked. "Why would I tell anybody anything? That's what I told him, and that's what I'm tellin' you guys."

Two men entered the saloon and looked toward Canaday's table.

"I got to take some bets, fellas," Canaday said, lowering his voice. "Honest, I never told Adams nothing."

Best and Dennis exchanged a glance, and then Dennis said "Okay. Keep it that way, Jim."

The two men turned and left the saloon, and then the other men approached the table with money in hand. Canaday took a moment to wonder why everybody picked today to threaten him, and then started quoting odds to the two bettors.

TWENTY-EIGHT

Clint spent a good part of the rest of the day sleeping because he planned to be awake for as much of the game as possible. It was eleven-thirty when he entered the saloon and most of the players were crowded into the place. He saw Bat and Luke standing at the bar, each holding a beer, and went over to join them. Ben Dillon came over when he spotted him.

"Beer?"

"Please," Clint said. "Aren't you supposed to be upstairs?"

"We'll open that bar when the game starts."

"Where are our hosts?" Clint asked, accepting the beer.

"I think they're in Mr. Ordway's office," Dillon said. "Gonna come out in about fifteen minutes to start moving people upstairs."

"I assume my man is still up there?"

"I brought him a beer and he like to shot my head off," Dillon complained.

Clint had arranged for old man O'Brien to send some food up for Horne. He asked Dillon if the food had been brought over.

"Brought over and picked up," Dillon said.

"Good," Clint said, and turned to his friends. "You both look well rested."

"Rested and ready to go," Bat said.

"Who sets the tables up?" Luke asked. "Ordway? Dick Clark?"

"I don't know," Clint said. "I'm not involved in that part of things. My guess is they won't want to sit you two at the same table in the beginning. Wouldn't want one of you knocking the other one out."

"Why not?" Bat asked. "Sounds look a good strategy to me."

"Well," Clint said, "maybe if Ordway or Clark were playing in the game, but they're not. They'll probably want to keep the top players in for a while."

"Why is Clark not playing?" Bat asked.

"He doesn't think it would be ethical," Clint said, "since he's running the game."

At that moment the door to Ordway's office opened and he stepped out with Dick Clark. Both men moved to the center of the room.

"Gentlemen," Dick Clark called out, "if we could ask you to move upstairs in an orderly fashion we can get this game started. I'll go up first so I can direct you to your tables."

With that Clark went upstairs and Ordway started to talk.

"We have a small bar upstairs for players, and some of our girls will be serving drinks at the tables. If you want to take a five-minute break you can do it at the upstairs bar. Hopefully you're all well rested because this game will continue until someone wins. You have to have the best cards, and stay awake."

That drew a laugh from the assembled players. Clint

noticed that there was not one woman in the group. He knew of a few women who could have competed—and afforded to compete—in the game, but they had either chosen not to, or didn't know about the game.

"All right gents, let's go up two by two and get seated."

Clint watched as the players trooped up the steps.

"See you later," Bat said, and he and Luke went up at the end of the line. Ordway came over to stand by Clint at the bar.

"Up you go, Ben," he said to Dillon.

"Yes, sir."

Ben Dillon left the bar to the young man who had been hired to replace him downstairs.

"What about you, John?" Clint asked. "You going to watch the beginning of the game?"

"Oh, yeah, I'll watch for a while, but I'll be more interested in watching toward the end."

"Will you be bringing in food for the players?"

"Yes," Ordway said, "we'll lay some food out on the small bar upstairs and give them breaks so they can eat."

"That's good."

"What do you say we go up?"

"Lead the way."

When they got upstairs most of the players were seated. Clint could see that Bat, Luke and Ben Thompson had all been seated in the main room but at different tables. He walked over to where Horne was standing at the safe.

"Ready for a break, Art?"

"Actually I'm okay," Horne said. "I'd like to stay and watch for a while."

"Okay," Clint said. "I'm going to check the other rooms."

He went out into the hall and saw Dillon behind the temporary bar.

"Got enough room back there?"

"Actually, it's okay."

Clint could see that. The bar was about six feet long, plenty of room for Ben Dillon.

"I'm going to have a look at the other rooms," Clint said.

"Want a beer on the way back?"

"No," Clint said, "I can't be drinking all night. I'll be fine."

"Suit yourself."

Clint went to the other rooms and took a look inside. The games had started, and everyone was engrossed in their cards. He went back to the first room and found the same.

The competition for over a million dollars was on.

TWENTY-NINE

Clint spent most of his time out in the hall, talking to Ben Dillon, occasionally looking into one room or another. As players busted out of the game they'd stop at the temporary bar for a drink, and then move on down the stairs.

Stacy and Trudy were working the rooms as waitresses, taking drinks from the bar to the tables. Later in the night, after the game had been going for a few hours, Andy appeared bearing trays of sandwiches that old man O'Brien had donated.

"Good morning," she said to Clint, bumping his hip with hers.

" 'Morning," he said. "Are you just the sandwich lady or are you here to work?"

"Oh, I'm working," she said. She took off the wrap she was wearing to reveal the low-cut front of her dress. Her breasts looked as if they were going to fall out.

"Wow," he said.

"Thanks. I have to go to work now, but will I see you later?"

"Not until after the game," Clint said.

"But they said it could go on for three days!"

"Sorry."

She pouted, but then smiled and went to work.

The sandwiches were gone in two hours, and so was the third room and half the second. Clint figured by daybreak they'd be down to the main room.

He let Horne go to his room to get some sleep, but the younger man promised to be back early.

"I don't need that much sleep," Horne assured him.

Clint remained in the hall until the second room was shut down and the entire game was taking place in the main room. Then he was able to move into the room and watch the action. The sun wasn't even up yet.

By morning they were down to eight tables. Bat, Luke and Ben Thompson were still in the game, and still at separate tables. John McNee was still alive, as were Lucky Slim Johnson and Canadian Jack.

At eight A.M. Andy and Trudy left and came back with a batch of biscuits and eggs. Stacy remained behind because, despite the early hour, some of the players were still drinking.

Clint had not seen Bat or Luke take a drink for the past few hours. Both men seemed to take a break at the same time by design in order to get some breakfast. When they reached the door Clint went out into the hall with them. They found not only the eggs and biscuits on the bar but some bacon and coffee, as well.

"How are you fellas doing?" Clint asked. He had cut two of the biscuits in half and filled them full of eggs and bacon.

"I'm the chip leader at my table," Bat said, "but I don't really have any competition there."

"I'm pretty close," Luke said. "I've got Lucky at my table and he's doing well."

"How's he holding up?" Clint asked.

"Pretty good, in spite of the fact he's at death's door and has been drinkin' all night."

"I don't know how he's doin' it," Bat said around a mouthful of eggs and bacon.

Clint poured himself some coffee and washed down his food with it.

"This come from that same place?" Luke asked.

"Yep."

"Good food," Bat said. "Time to get back to it."

He and Luke went back inside and Clint remained at the bar. Dick Clark came out of the room and approached Clint.

"Breakfast?" Clint asked.

"Just some coffee."

Clint poured him a cup.

"We got rid of those other rooms pretty quick," Clark said. "Now the players seem to be more evenly matched and are holding their own."

"It'll be that way for a while until someone starts getting hot," Clint said.

"I'm kind of sorry I decided not to play," Clark said.

"Is it too late to pay the entry fee and sit in?"

"Oh yeah," Clark said. "That wouldn't be fair to the players who are already out of the game."

"I never knew you had so many scruples, Dick."

"I'm developing more and more in my old age, I think," the man complained.

"Not really good for a gambler, is it?"

"Not at all."

The three girls came over to the bar and looked at Clark, who took the hint.

"Okay, ladies, we'll only need one of you for a while," he said. "You can decide which one among you."

"I'll stay," Andy said. "You girls have been up longer than I have."

Trudy and Stacy promised to be back in four hours.

"I'll see if anyone wants coffee at their table," Andy said, and went back into the room.

"Well," Clark said, "things seem to be working out well. At least nobody's tried to hijack the game."

Clint waited a beat, then said, "Yet."

THIRTY

The voices of the dealers mingled with the voices of the players as the day wore on. Clint listened to the talk from his friend's tables to hear how they were doing. More often than not he heard . . .

"The play is to Mr. Masterson . . ."
"Raise . . ."
"Call . . ."
"I fold . . ."
"Call . . ."
"Hand to Mr. Masterson."

Or . . .
"The play is on Mr. Short."
"Bet a hundred . . ."
"Call . . ."
"Raise . . ."
"Fold . . ."
"I raise . . ."
"Call . . ."
"Hand to Mr. Short."

•   •   •

And the same kinds of things were happening at Ben Thompson's table, as well.

By the time they got to the dinner break, Dick Clark had decided to turn one of the other rooms into a dining room for the players, and they had meals brought up from O'Brien's café.

"Old man O'Brien is really being supportive of this game, isn't he?" Clint asked Dick Clark at one point.

"Yes, he is," Clark said. "I guess he thinks this'll be good for the town and, ultimately, for his business."

The players took turns leaving their tables and eating, but only one or two players from each table at the time, so that the games would continue.

Clint had apparently done a good job hiring the dealers, because there had not been a hint of trouble in that department. All the players seemed satisfied with the way the cards were being dealt.

Clint managed to have dinner with Bat Masterson when his friend took his dinner break, while Luke Short continued to play.

"How's it looking at the other tables?" Bat asked. "I can't really keep track as easily as I did when the game began. The players at my table now are much better than the earlier ones."

The weaker players had been picked off and weaned out of the game by now.

"Luke seems to be slowly but surely cleaning the men at his table out," Clint said.

"What about Slim?"

"He's the reason Luke is doing it slowly," Clint said. "Lucky Slim seems to be his only competition."

"What about the other tables?"

"Most of them seem evenly matched," Clint said, "waiting for someone to get hot—except for Ben's table. He seems to have that one pretty well in hand."

"Looks like I'll end up at a table with Thompson and Luke."

"Brady and Bret are ahead, but they're at the same table and might be canceling each other out."

"Good," Bat said. "I don't want to have to end up facing them and Luke at the same time."

Bat pushed his plate away, his steak only partially consumed.

"Not going to finish?" Clint asked.

"I can't enjoy it," Bat said. "I just wanted to eat enough to take the edge off my hunger." He stood up. "I've got to get back to my table before—like you said—somebody else gets hot."

"Good luck."

Bat left the room and Clint finished his own steak. Horne had returned a couple of hours before, and was now watching the room—and the safe—while Clint ate.

Stacy and Trudy had returned, as well, and Andy was now off getting her beauty sleep. Clint didn't know where Ordway was at the moment, but he expected the man to appear to take a look and see who was left in the game.

A duty that had fallen to him that he hadn't expected was picking up the money each dealer was raking in from the pots at their respective tables. From time to time he'd go around and collect, and, since Dick Clark knew the combination to the safe, they would open it up and put the money in. Clint didn't like opening the safe that many times. Anybody with a gun could have stood up at any time to try to rob the safe. It didn't happen, but each time they opened the safe, Clint was ready. It was either that or put the extra money in John Ordway's office. Although it wasn't a million dollars, it was starting to add up.

Think of the devil, Clint thought, as John Ordway walked into the makeshift dining room. At that moment Clint was alone, but other players would soon be filing in to eat.

"I had a look in the room," Ordway said. "Players are dropping faster than I thought."

"Not really," Clint said. "Most of the ones who were eliminated already were gone before morning. It's pretty much leveled out since then."

"Well," Ordway said, "this was a good idea. Better than having the players eat out in the hall. I should have thought of this earlier."

"Dick's got to earn his keep with a good idea now and then," Clint joked.

"Believe me," Ordway said, showing no sense of humor, "Dick Clark earns his keep."

"Glad to hear it."

A couple of players entered the room, then, including Luke Short.

"Let me get out of here and give them room to eat," Ordway said. "Has the raked money been going into the safe?"

"Like clockwork."

"Good," Ordway said. "I knew having you handle security was the right move."

"Thanks."

"No," Ordway said. "Thank you."

As he left, Luke came over carrying his plate of what was now a lukewarm steak.

"What's he beaming about?" he asked, joining Clint at the table.

"Things are going the way he planned, apparently."

"Going the way I planned, too," Luke said, "at least at my table. What's going on at the others?"

From that point on, Clint had essentially the same conversation with Luke Short he'd just had with Bat Masterson.

THIRTY-ONE

In another part of town, in a small saloon, two men were meeting. One had just arrived in town early that morning after having ridden all night. His name was Arlo Catcher. The second man was known to Catcher by the name Mr. Brown.

"You couldn't have timed your arrival any better," Mr. Brown told Catcher. "The entire town is focused on this game. That means hardly anyone gave you any notice when you rode in."

Catcher sat up straight. He was a man who liked to be noticed. If he hadn't been covered with trail dust at the moment, he would have been impeccably turned out. His beard and mustache, even on the trail, were kept very neat and cleanly trimmed. Even his trail clothes were made of the finest fabric, and would return to their former finery when laundered. If not, they would be discarded and he would buy new clothing.

The gun on his hip was well-oiled and fully loaded. It was pearl-handled and engraved with the letter *C*.

"I'm not used to going unnoticed," he said.

"Yes, I understand that."

"If you wanted someone people wouldn't notice," Catcher said, "you hired the wrong man."

"No," Mr. Brown said, "I have hired the right man for the job I want done."

"And what is that job?"

"There is over a million dollars in a safe in a saloon in Old Town," Mr. Brown said, "across the dead line."

"Because of the poker game you mentioned?"

"That's right."

Catcher sat back. There was a cup of coffee in front of him, but he hadn't touched it. After this meeting he was going to go and have a cold beer.

"A game that size has got to attract the top names," he said.

"You're right," Brown said. "Bat Masterson is over there, as are Luke Short and Ben Thompson . . . and security is being handled by Clint Adams."

"The Gunsmith?"

"In fact," Brown went on, "he is the only security, that I know of, except for one other man he's hired to assist him."

"And do I know that man?" Catcher asked. "Did he resurrect Wild Bill for the job?"

"The second man will be of no concern to you," Brown said. "And neither will the players."

"Got to be a ton of them over there."

"That's why we won't make a move on the safe until the game is down to the last three or four players. There's every possibility that the final three or four will not include Mr. Masterson or Mr. Short or Mr. Thompson. Poker is a game of luck, and perhaps they won't have it."

"Poker's a game of skill and luck, Mr. Brown," Catcher said. "Obviously you've never played."

"I prefer other games, Mr. Catcher," Brown said, "and other gambles."

"Do I have any assistance in this thing?" Catcher asked.

"I have two men working for me, keeping an eye on the game and the main principals," Brown said, "but they are idiots. You may bring in whatever men you like."

"And how long do I have to collect these men?"

"I would say two days, at the most."

"Not much time."

"Frankly," Brown said, "being acquainted with your reputation, I didn't think you would need that much help."

"Oh sure," Catcher said, "I'll just go up against Adams and Masterson and Short and Thompson all by myself."

"As I said," Brown replied, "they may not all be there in the end."

"I think I'd do well to assume that most of them will," Catcher said.

"Am I to understand that your reputation is unearned? Or . . . possibly exaggerated?"

"If you knew anything about reputations, Mr. Brown," Catcher said, "you'd know that they're all exaggerated— even the four men we're discussing now haven't done all the things they're reputed to have done. But they've done enough of them, and so have I."

Brown waited for Catcher to speak, feeling like a fisherman with a baited hook in the water.

"All right," Catcher said, "give me as many details as you can. . . ."

After Mr. Brown had told Catcher as much as he knew about the game, the players and the layout, he asked, "Would you like something colder than that to drink?"

"As a matter of fact, I would."

Mr. Brown got up, went to the bar and came back with an ice-cold mug of beer. Catcher lifted it to his mouth, and when he set it down there was only about a quarter of a mug left.

"All right, Mr. Catcher," Brown said, "you have all the facts. Is this something you think you'd like to be involved in?"

"Mr. Brown," Arlo Catcher said, "with all of the personalities you've told me are already involved, this is something I would kill to be involved in."

THIRTY-TWO

A couple of players got real hot and cleared their tables by nightfall. One of them was Ben Thompson, and the other was Luke Short, who cleared everyone off his table except for Lucky Slim. As a result, Slim, Thompson and Luke Short ended up at the same table, and the tables were now down to five. Forty players for the jackpot in the safe.

Two other tables had been consolidated and Bat was now matching aces and eights with John McNee from England and Canadian Jack, among others.

The games were getting real interesting, which is why Clint, Horne, Dick Clark and John Ordway were in the room watching. Ben Dillon came in every so often to watch and see if anyone wanted a drink, because all three girls had been sent home to get some sleep.

For the most part, though, the players were deep into their games and had stopped drinking—all but Big Ed Cooley. He had been drinking since the game started, and Clint wondered how he could even see his cards. He had been doing very well for himself, though—until lately.

His last few hands had not gone well and had cut into his stack of chips.

"Goddamnit!" he shouted, throwing his cards across the table. "I hate losing to a kicker!"

He'd just had a pair of aces but had lost to another pair of aces backed by a king kicker.

Clint knew it was a rough way to lose a hand, matching pairs but losing to the kicker.

"Where's that goddamned girl?" he shouted.

Ben Dillon came over. "Would you like another drink, sir?"

Ed looked up at Dillon, and although he was able to see his cards he looked as if he was having trouble focusing on Dillon's face.

"Who're you?"

"I'm the bartender, sir."

"I don't want the bartender," Ed said. "I want that blond gal."

"That'd be Stacy, sir," Dillon said, "and she's gone home to get some rest."

"She's asleep?"

"That's right, sir, but I could—"

"Wake her up!" Ed Cooley shouted. "I wanna drink from the blond-haired gal."

"The bet is to you, sir," the dealer said to Big Ed.

"What?"

"The play is to you," the dealer said. "You have an ace. You're high on the table."

"You dealt while I was talking to the bartender?" Big Ed demanded. "You dealt while I wasn't looking?"

"Sir," the dealer said, "you didn't call for time to—"

"I was talkin' to the goddamned bartender!" Big Ed shouted.

"Ed," Ben Thompson said, 'take it easy." He and Luke were sitting at the same table with Cooley.

While they watched, Dick Clark leaned over to Clint and said, "This is where taking their guns away from them would have come in handy."

"When you have the kinds of reps some of these men have," Clint said, "you can't ask them to give up their guns."

"Are you going to do something?"

Clint didn't answer. Instead he looked at Horne, who leaned toward him.

"Stand by the safe while I try to defuse this."

"Right."

Horne moved over in front of the safe while Clint walked over to Big Ed Cooley's table.

"Ed . . ." he began.

Cooley looked up at him and squinted.

"Adams?"

"That's right."

"I want a redeal," he demanded. "He dealt out the cards while I wasn't lookin."

"Ed," Clint said, "It's your responsibility to watch the table."

"I was tryin' to get a drink!"

"Look," Clint said, "the bartender will get you a drink. Meanwhile, play your ace. You're high on the table, man."

"Yeah," Big Ed said, "I was high on the table before and look what happened. I lost to a king kicker."

"Ed," Clint said, "you've got to play your ace or fold. You're holding up the game."

"I ain't gettin' a new deal?"

"No."

He thought about that for a while.

"And I ain't gettin' a drink from the yellow-haired gal?"

"No," Clint said, "she's asleep."

The other players at the table were staring at the big man impatiently, waiting for him to make a decision.

"Well . . ." Ed said. He looked down at the ace, then up at the bartender, and then over at Clint.

"Ed . . ." Clint said, warningly. He didn't like what he was seeing in the big man's eyes. "Don't . . ."

"I got to . . ." Ed said.

"Got to what?" Clint asked.

Cooley looked up at Clint and said, "I got to break somethin'—or somebody."

"Then you'll have to fold your ace and do it outside, Ed," Clint said. "If you try to do that in here I'll have to stop you."

They matched stares for a moment and then Big Ed smiled and turned over his ace.

"I fold."

"About time," Ben Thompson.

Big Ed stood up, towering over the table, and over Clint.

"You and me, Adams," he said. "Outside."

Clint sighed and said, "After you, Ed."

As Big Ed Cooley walked away from the table Clint looked at the dealer.

"How much has he got left?"

The man looked at Clint and said, "He would have busted out in this hand if he'd lost."

Clint nodded, then turned and followed Big Ed Cooley out into the hall.

"Big Ed's done," Luke Short said.

"Ed will bust Adams in half and be back for his last hand," Thompson said.

"Wanna bet?" Short asked.

Thompson considered the offer for a few moments, then asked, "What odds?"

THIRTY-THREE

Horne, Clark and Ordway watched as the big man walked past them with a big grin on his face. When Clint came by, Horne stopped him.

"You need help?" he asked.

"Don't worry."

"Are you going to kill him?" Clark asked.

"What's he done to deserve killing?" Clint asked. Then he looked at Horne. "I'll probably need you in a few minutes, but I'll come in and relieve you, first."

"Okay."

As Clint followed Big Ed out the door, Ordway asked Clark, "What's he going to do?"

"Damned if I know," the gambler answered.

From his table Bat Masterson briefly considered folding his hand and following his friend into the hall to help him with Big Ed Cooley, but before he did he looked at his hole card again. It was still an ace, and there were two more on the table in front of him with his fifth card still to follow.

He decided that Clint Adams could handle Ed Cooley all by himself.

Likewise, Luke Short thought of helping Clint but decided that his friend might take offense. Besides, he now had a pair of kings on the table in front of him.

Ben Thompson never considered helping Clint. He was too busy looking across the table at Luke Short's kings, wondering if the cagey little gambler had another in the hole. He himself had a pair of aces—one visible, one not—and was wondering if he should call the pair of kings that were on the table, or raise.

Clint followed Big Ed out into the hall, and when he got there noticed that the man had gotten distracted by the bar, which Ben Dillon was now standing behind. It was a plank bar and probably would not have stood the pressure if Big Ed had leaned on it.

Clint quickly decided on the best way to handle a man the size of Ed Cooley when that man was intent on breaking something, or somebody.

"When is the blonde comin' back, I said—" Cooley was snapping at Dillon when Clint approached him from behind.

Dillon looked past Cooley at Clint and before Big Ed could react, Clint took the man's gun from his holster and coldcocked him with his own weapon. He did not want to risk denting the frame of his own gun on the big fella's head.

Cooley stiffened, then turned and stared at Clint, who thought he was going to have to hit him again. Finally, though, the man started to fall toward him, and instead of trying to catch him and break his fall, Clint simply stepped out of the way. Cooley hit with a *thud* that shook the entire second floor.

"Hold this," Clint said, handing Dillon the gun. "If he wakes up, hit him again."

"I don't want to kill him," Dillon said.

"Then don't hit him the same place I did," Clint said.

When he reentered the room, most of the players ignored him. Bat had not improved on his three aces, but they had been enough to give him the pot. He did notice that Clint had come back safe and sound, and turned his attention to the next hand.

Luke and Thompson noticed Clint coming back because their hand had also resolved itself. Luke did, in fact, have a third king in the hole, but Thompson had pulled a third ace on the last card and had taken the hand. It put him just about on even terms with Luke for the most chips on the table.

"What happ—" Clark started to ask as Clint went by, but Clint held up a hand to stop him.

He walked over to the table Big Ed had been playing at, looked at the dealer and said, "Close him out. He's done."

"What about his chips?" the dealer asked. "He's got a few hundred dollars left."

Clint thought a moment, then said, "Push them into the next pot."

The dealer had never heard of such a thing, but said, "Okay. Whatever you say."

Clint nodded, turned and walked over to where Clark, Ordway and Art Horne were standing in front of the safe.

"Art, go out into the hall and help Dillon carry Big Ed downstairs, if the two of you can handle him."

"And then what?"

"When you get down there send someone for the sheriff. When he gets here tell him Mr. Ordway would like the man to spend the night in jail to sober up. If the sheriff wants to talk to Mr. Ordway first, send him up here."

"No need for that," Ordway said. "I'll help them carry the big man downstairs, and then wait to talk to the sheriff myself. The three of us should be able to handle him."

"Okay," Clint said.

Ordway looked at Clint and said, "That was well handled."

"That's what you hired me for."

Ordway nodded, and he and Art Horne went out into the hall.

"How badly did you hurt him?" Clark asked.

"I coldcocked him," Clint said. "I wasn't about to fight him, and I didn't want to kill him. He'll wake up in the morning with a double hangover, one from the booze and one from the bump."

"Not exactly the way I expected any of the players to bust out of the game."

"He was about done, anyway," Clint said. "That's probably why he was ready to start a fight."

"Well," Clark said, "like John said, that was really well handled."

"That kind of trouble is better than the other kind we're expecting, isn't it?" Clint asked.

"Are we actually expecting the other kind?"

"I am," Clint said. "And so are you, or you wouldn't have hired me for the job."

THIRTY-FOUR

The rest of the day passed without incident. Several other players busted out of the game and the number of tables was reduced to four. Darkness came, and the girls returned to serve drinks. Once again O'Brien donated dinners for the players. But probably half as many as he'd donated the night before.

Unlike the night before, where they had taken a break for dinner separately, Bat and Luke broke at the same time, so they sat and had steaks with Clint. Art Horne was once again on guard in front of the safe.

"This game is not going to last as long as some people thought," Bat said.

"I agree," Luke said. "I didn't think we'd be down to four tables this quickly."

"Looks like all the top players have made it this far, though," Clint said. "Players might start dropping out pretty grudgingly, if you know what I mean."

"I know exactly what you mean," Luke Short said around a mouthful of beef. "I'll leave this game feet-first."

"You know," Bat said, "it might have been better if

they'd split the prize money, say, three ways, instead of making it winner-take-all."

"Why, Bat," Luke said, "are you starting to have doubts about the outcome of this game?"

"Not at all," Bat said. "I'm just starting to feel sorry that you're going to walk away from this game empty-handed."

"Oh, really?" Luke asked, laughing. "So you'd be willing to split the pot with me?"

"You mean," Bat asked, "make a deal now? Whichever one of us wins we split the money?"

"That's an interesting idea," Clint said. "I wonder how many other players have formed an alliance?"

"Well," Luke said, "we haven't formed one, yet."

"Do either of you have the slightest doubt that you're the one who's going to win?"

Bat and Luke exchanged a glance.

"Or maybe you just don't want to say."

"Well," Luke said, "I suppose there's a chance Bat might win."

"Or Luke," Bat added.

"I think there's a good chance that if one of you doesn't win, the other will," Clint said. "But I also think anything can happen. After all, there is an element of luck involved in poker, isn't there?"

Bat and Luke both looked at Clint as if he were crazy.

His two friends went back to the game without a deal definitely being struck. Clint was about to leave, too, when Ben Thompson walked in, followed by John McNee. The Englishman nodded to Clint and went to eat his dinner. Thompson, however, fetched his plate and joined Clint at his table.

"Adams," he said.

"Hello, Ben."

"Have a cup of coffee with me?"

"Sure."

Clint poured his own cup and Thompson's cup full.

"Pretty slick the way you handled Big Ed without killin' him," the gambler said.

"Thanks. I didn't really see any reason to kill him. I just wanted to get him away from the game and give him someplace to sleep it off."

"So where is he?"

"By now, jail, I hope."

"That's good," Thompson said. "A jail cell just might hold him."

"To what do I owe this invitation, Ben?" Clint asked.

"I was wonderin' about your friends."

"I have lots of friends."

"I mean Masterson and Luke," Thompson said.

"Ah," Clint said, "and what were you wondering?"

"Seems to me it would be a good idea for those two to form an alliance."

"An alliance to do what?"

"Split the prize money, of course," Thompson said. "There's plenty to go around."

"Is that what you've done, Ben?" Clint asked. "Made a deal with someone to split the money?"

"I've thought about it," Thompson said, cutting off a hunk of meat and stuffing it into his mouth. He was eating in a hurry so he could get back to the game, pausing only to speak.

Clint sat back and regarded the man critically for a moment, trying to read him.

"What?" Thompson asked.

"I get it."

"Get what?"

"You're thinking of forming an alliance with some-one," Clint said, "and you'd prefer it to be Bat or Luke. Other than you, you think they're the best players in the room."

"Well . . . aren't they?"

"Probably," Clint said, "but I doubt Bat would make such a deal with you."

"Has he made one with Luke?"

"I wouldn't know."

Thompson thought a moment, chewing.

"So you think my best bet is Luke."

"I didn't say that, either."

"Well, if they haven't made a deal with each other, there's no one else in that room they would have made one with."

"That's your observation."

"You have no opinion?"

"No."

Thompson smiled.

"You're the only other person they'd make a deal with, and you're not playing."

Clint chose not to respond.

Thompson finished chewing, washed it down with a slurp of coffee, and pushed the plate away.

"I thought since they took this break together they might have talked about it."

No reply.

"They did, didn't they?" Thompson asked.

No response.

"That's okay," the other man said, standing. "I think I found out what I wanted."

"Not from me."

Ben Thompson tipped his hat to Clint and left the room.

"Alliances?"

Clint turned at the sound of John McNee's British accent.

"Hello, John."

"Clint. Mind if I join you for a cup?"

"Come ahead," Clint said. "Everybody else has already."

McNee carried his cup over to Clint's table, leaving his plate behind. The Englishman was in his forties, impeccably dressed. He was a handsome man, and Clint knew from past experience that he did very well with the ladies—and with cards.

"How are you doing in there?" Clint asked.

"Holding my own, I suppose," McNee said. "There are some bloody good players in the room."

"I know there are."

"But forming alliances, splitting the prize money," McNee said, "that doesn't quite sound cricket to me."

"Well, it hasn't happened as far as I know," Clint said. "If anyone has formed any partnerships, I don't know about it."

"Well, that's good to hear." He finished his coffee and stood up, but before leaving looked down at Clint. "Tell me something?"

"What?"

"If I were to want to partner with someone," McNee said, "who would you suggest?"

Clint grinned and said, "Sorry, John. I can't help you."

THIRTY-FIVE

A couple of more gamblers entered the room but Clint
got up and made for the door before he could be caught
again. He wondered, now that they were down to four
tables, if the idea of forming an alliance was going
around?

He stopped at the makeshift bar and said to Dillon,
"Let me have a beer, Ben."

"Wow," Dillon said, "you haven't had one in a while."

"I'm just thirsty," Clint said. "Been doing a lot of talking."

"About what?" Dillon asked, putting a beer in front of
him.

"Never mind," Clint said, picking up the beer. "It's not
very important."

Clint sipped his beer and studied the bartender, surprised to see him looking so awake.

"Why don't you look sleepy?" Clint asked. "You
haven't had any rest, have you?"

"Catnaps behind the bar," Dillon said, "but I really
don't sleep that much. What about you?"

"I'm used to going without sleep," Clint said. "When

this is all over I'll go down for half a day or so. I'm finding this whole thing too interesting to miss."

Dillon frowned.

"What's happening that I don't know about?" he asked. "Just looks like a card game to me."

"Things are starting to happen behind the scenes," Clint said.

"Like what?"

"I probably should tell your boss before I tell you." On the other hand, maybe there was nothing to tell. If players wanted to make deals with each other to split the money, what was wrong with that?

Clint finished his beer and said, "Nothing's really happened yet. If something does, then I'll talk to Ordway and Clark. For now, I think I'll go in and relieve Art. Unlike us, he does need to get some sleep."

Dillon shrugged and watched Clint Adams walk off. Whatever he had on his mind was none of his business, anyway. His job was to pour drinks and that was all—for now.

Clint went into the poker room. His eyes felt like they'd never close again. He stood just inside the door, looking out over the four tables and it was as if he could hear each card as it left the dealer's hand and hit the table. He knew what he'd said was true; when this was all over, he'd have to collapse for a while, but right now he felt as if he could stay awake for days.

He went over to Art Horne, who was standing in front of the safe but was watching the play at Bat Masterson's table.

"Looks like Masterson is about to get rid of another player," Horne said to Clint, "or bust out of the game himself."

The play was down to two players, Bat and a man named Brady, who was considered a hell of a gambler. From the looks of it both Bat and Brady had all their money in the pot. That meant that whoever lost the hand was out of the game. Both men were facing elimination.

Bat had a two, three, four, and five on the table in mixed suits. Brady had three sixes. This was going to come down to sheer luck, because there was no bluffing at this point.

"Pot's right," the dealer said. "Mr. Brady is called."

Brady hesitated, then turned over his hole card. It didn't match, so he still had three sixes.

Bat turned over his hole card and it was an ace, giving him a straight. Brady stood up, shook hands with Bat, and then went out into the hall for a beer.

"Those aces," Clint said, shaking his head, "they find Bat wherever he is."

"Wow," Horne said, "that was close."

"Not really," Clint said. "Bat knew he had him."

"How?"

"Somehow he just knows," Clint said. "That's what makes him so good."

"But I thought Brady was supposed to be one of the best gamblers around."

"He is," Clint said. "Bat's just better."

At that point Bat Masterson looked up, caught Clint's eyes while raking in his chips, and winked. By getting rid of Brady he'd eliminated one of his biggest hurdles to winning. The others were Luke, Ben Thompson, John McNee and Lucky Slim, all of whom had stacks of chips in front of them.

Clint could see that if they consolidated players now they could get down to three tables, but Clark—who was watching at the moment from across the room—was apparently satisfied to let the tables go with six players each, for the time being.

"Only twenty-four players left," Horne said. "How long do you think it'll take?"

"Hard to say," Clint said. "So far, it's gone much faster than anyone imagined it would. You want to go and get some sleep?"

"Naw," Horne said. "I'm good. These games are startin' to get real interestin'."

Clint agreed. He folded his arms and watched the dealer dole the cards out to Bat and the others on what he had come to think of as table number one. . . .

In Old Town, in the same small saloon, Mr. Brown looked across the table at Arlo Catcher.

"There's a problem," he said.

"What's that?"

"The game is going faster than we'd anticipated."

Catcher decided not to ask who "we" were.

"Have you managed to recruit your help?" the older man asked.

"No," Catcher said. "I sent some telegrams but no one would get here in time—and now that you tell me the game is going quickly, I guess that's out. I'll have to make do with your two men."

"Ah. You've met Mr. Best and Mr. Dennis," Mr. Brown said. "What do you think of them?"

"Like you said," Catcher replied, "they're idiots—but they'll do what they're told."

"Oh, yes. And have you looked over Mr. Ordway's operation?"

"Downstairs, yes," Catcher said.

"And? Can you get upstairs?"

"I believe so."

"Do you know who is still in the game?" Brown asked. "Because if you don't I've had someone—"

"Everyone in that saloon knows who's still in the game," Catcher said. "Masterson, Short and Thompson are still up there."

"And Adams, of course," Brown said.

"Right. The word I got is there's still twenty-four players."

"Yes, that's the information I have."

"I'll need to wait until they get down to one table," Catcher said. "Even I'm not dumb enough to go up against twenty-four poker players—especially when I'm trying to steal their prize money."

"Well," Brown said, "the way things are going they may be down to one table by later tonight."

"That'd be fine," Catcher said. "I wouldn't mind doing this job in the dark."

Mr. Brown sat back in his chair.

"This will work, you know," he said. "Even if those men all make it to the final table."

"Uh-huh."

The two men regarded each other for a few moments.

"I can get you two or three more men, if you like," Brown said. "Of course, they'll have no specific talents— except for being able to hold guns."

"I'll let you know if I need a couple of more gun holders," Catcher said. "For now let's just leave things the way they are." He stood up. "I'll be going back to the saloon now. I'll let you know what happens."

"Please do," Brown said. "After all, this is my operation."

Catcher stopped and looked at him.

"For want of a better word," Brown added.

THIRTY-SIX

Arlo Catcher entered the saloon, saw Joe Best and Hank Dennis sitting at a table watching the stairs to the second floor. The only job they had right now was counting the men who came down those stairs.

Catcher went to the bar for a beer, then turned and surveyed the room. He didn't go and sit with the two men because he didn't want anyone connecting them.

The man he knew as Mr. Brown was supplying him with two opportunities. First, the opportunity to make a lot of money. Second, the chance to make a big name for himself, taking down a game in which Bat Masterson, Luke Short, Ben Thompson and Clint Adams were all involved. When the word got out about what he'd done, he'd be the biggest legend in the West.

But he also had the feeling something was wrong. Mr. Brown was not telling him everything, of that he was sure. Under any other circumstances he would have passed on this job, but the opportunities were just too plentiful, and too important. He just had to accomplish it while being assisted by two idiots, and paid by a man he didn't trust.

* * *

Another player stood up from Bat's table, shook hands all around and then left.

"Bat's table is down to five," Horne said. "The others still all have six."

Clint simply nodded. Bat was playing the best poker he'd seen in some time. If he were going to bet, he would have put all his money on Bat at that moment.

Dick Clark came over and stood next to him.

"I've been watching Luke," he said. "He can't lose, right now."

"Bat's playing perfect poker," Clint said.

"Care to make a side wager?" Clark asked. "I'll take Luke."

Clint shook his head.

"They're both my friends," he said. "I don't think I want to choose one over the other."

"Take Ben Thompson, then," Clark suggested. "He's also playing very well."

"Two more players are leaving," Clint said, inclining his head. "I think you're down to twenty-one players—four at Bat's table and five at that one over there."

"I guess I'll have to even it up," Clark said. "Seven players at each table."

"Seven's an odd number," Horne pointed out. Clint and Dick Clark both turned to look at him. "Well, it is."

"I just meant I'll move them around to put the same number of players at each table."

"Oh," Horne said.

Once Dick Clark had moved the players around, Clint noticed that Bat, Luke, and Ben Thompson were at separate tables. John McNee was seated at Luke's table, and Lucky Slim was playing opposite Ben Thompson.

Other than Bat, Luke and Thompson, it was Lucky

Slim Johnson who had the most chips. He also looked like death warmed over, but then he had looked that way when the game had started.

Clint decided to watch Slim for a while, and saw that the man was playing as well as he ever had. Every so often he turned away to cough into a handkerchief, but he never seemed to allow his ailment to interfere with the game. No one had to wait for him. He made his plays on cue, and he made them well.

Bat and Luke definitely had some competition in Lucky Slim Johnson—probably the only man Clint had ever known who had two nicknames.

THIRTY-SEVEN

"Thirteen," Joe Best said.

"Fourteen," Hank Dennis said.

"I counted thirteen."

"And I counted fourteen," Dennis insisted.

Best frowned.

"So what are we gonna tell Mr. Catcher when he comes back?" he asked.

Dennis stared at his partner.

"Catcher's off gettin' his ashes hauled while we're here countin' heads," Dennis said. "What's the difference?"

Arlo Catcher looked down at the girl whose head was bobbing up and down in his lap. He'd asked the Madam if she had a girl who would do French, but he never expected it to be a Chinese girl named Lotus. She was sucking his swollen cock like it was a salt lick and she was a mule. He'd learned to like this sort of thing when he'd discovered it in a New Orleans whorehouse, but even those women didn't do it as good as this Chinese girl did.

Suddenly he rose up, lifting his butt off the bed as he exploded into her mouth and damned if that little gal didn't just gobble it all up without spilling a drop.

When she released his cock from her mouth she smiled up at him and asked, "Was that all right?"

She had the prettiest little mouth and the tiniest, prettiest little titties he'd ever seen.

"That was perfect, Lotus," he said.

"You like I do something else?"

"I would," he said, "but I don't think I've got the wherewithal, right now."

She smiled and said to him, "I give you wherewithal," and lowered her head, again. . . .

As Catcher dressed, the Chinese girl watched him from the bed, her hands busy between her own legs. She had just ridden him for half an hour, after giving him the "wherewithal" again, and still that wasn't enough for her?

"You're amazing," he said.

"More than you know," she said, without her Chinese accent.

"What happened to the accent?"

"That's for the suckers," she said. "You're not a sucker, are you?"

"No," he said, "I'm not."

"I can put the accent back on next time you come, though," she promised. "If you prefer."

"No," he said, "that's okay. I think I like you better this way. I should have been tipped off when you knew what the word *wherewithal* meant."

She smiled lasciviously and said, "I thought I just taught you what the word meant."

He smiled and strapped on his gun.

"Are you going to be using that while you're here?" she asked.

"Possibly."

"Think you'll be coming back?"

"Definitely."

She took her fingers away from her crotch, licked them, then put them back.

"I'll keep it warm for you, then."

"Jesus," he said, his pants swelling once again with the "wherewithal."

He got out of there while he still had it.

When Catcher got back to the saloon, Best and Dennis were still seated at their table. He went to the bar and ordered a beer. It was midday, and the place wasn't very full. He had an idea there were more men upstairs than downstairs.

While he was leaning on the bar drinking his beer, Joe Best came over and stood next to him.

"Beer," he said to the young bartender.

While he waited, he spoke to Catcher from the side of his mouth.

"I counted," he said, "and there should be thirteen men left upstairs."

"Uh-huh."

Best couldn't help it. It was eating at him than he and Dennis had a different count.

"Hank says fourteen, but I counted thirteen."

The bartender came and placed the beer in front of Best.

"If I went up there thinkin' there was thirteen men," Catcher said, "and there's fourteen, I could get killed."

"I thought you was gonna wait until there was only one table?" Best asked.

"I was just trying to make a point."

"What point?"

Without looking at Best, Catcher said, "That you and

your friend better find out exactly how many men are upstairs. I'm not movin' until I know that, and none of us is gettin' paid until I move. Understand?"

"I-I understand."

"Then go back to your table and tell you buddy."

"Yes, sir."

"Leave the beer," Catcher said. "You've already got one on the table."

"Yes, sir," Best said.

"Why the hell did you tell him we had different counts?" Hank Dennis demanded.

"I just couldn't—"

"Goddamnit!" Dennis swore. "He's got no right holdin' us up this way."

"Why don't you go and tell him that, Hank?"

"You got us into this mess," Dennis said, "and you're gonna get us out."

"How?"

"You're gonna find out how many men are upstairs."

"And how am I supposed to do that?" Best asked.

Dennis looked at him and said, "Ask!"

THIRTY-EIGHT

By the time dusk came around, they were down to two tables of five. Luke and Canadian Jack and Slim Johnson were at one table, Ben Thompson had been moved to Bat's.

Clint was starting to feel the effects of having been awake for so long.

"You look awful," John Ordway said. He had just returned late that afternoon. "Why don't you go into my room and lie down?"

"That's tempting," Clint said.

"I can handle this for a while," Horne told him. "And you yourself said that nothing will happen at least until we're down to one table."

Dick Clark was also present and added, "Go ahead, Clint. We'll wake you if anything comes up. Take a few hours."

They were right. He didn't think anything would happen until they were down to the last table. Anybody would be a fool to try anything, even until they were down to the final two or three players.

"Maybe an hour," Clint said. "Or two."

"I'll wake you in two," Clark said.

"Here's the key," Ordway said. "It's nice and quiet in there since you made me board up the windows."

Clint took the key.

A few things happened during that nap. . . .

Joe Best managed to catch Trudy as she came downstairs. She knew him from some other nights he had been in the saloon, and didn't mind talking to him. As a result, he found out exactly how many players were still in the game. He told Hank Dennis, who in turn told Arlo Catcher, who decided to remain in the saloon himself and keep count from that point on.

When the players got down to six at the last table, he knew. . . .

Soon after Clint went into Ordway's room for his nap, players began to drop like flies. Before long they were consolidated into one table that included Bat Masterson, Luke Short, John McNee, Ben Thompson, Canadian Jack and Lucky Slim Johnson.

Catcher, still standing at the bar, signaled for either Best or Dennis to come and join him.

"I'll go," Dennis said. "You've done enough damage."

Dennis went up, stood next to Catcher and ordered a beer.

"There are six players left," Catcher said to Dennis, who was surprised. He didn't know Catcher was counting on his own.

"I know."

"They include Bat Masterson, Luke Short and Ben Thompson."

"So?"

"Do you know any of them on sight?"

"I know Masterson."

"That's it?"

"Yes."

"Okay," Catcher said, "I know what they all look like. That means I don't need you fellas to keep watch anymore."

"What do you want us to do?"

"Go and tell your boss where we stand," he said, "and then come back."

"And do what?"

"Just be ready to cover me," Catcher said.

"We're not goin' up there with you?" Dennis asked.

"No," Catcher said.

"Won't you need help?"

"Don't worry," Catcher said. "Thanks to your boss I'll have all the help I need."

Dick Clark knocked on the door to Ordway's room and then entered. He found himself looking down the barrel of Clint Adams's gun.

"Just came in to wake you."

Clint lowered the gun and swung his legs to the floor. All he had removed for the nap was his gun belt and boots.

"I heard you." He reached down for his boots and started pulling them on. "Where do we stand?"

"We're down to one table," Clark said, "six players."

Clint looked at the man in surprise.

"That happened in two hours?"

"Well . . . I actually gave you three."

Clint stood up and strapped on his gun.

"You should have woken me up as soon as the game

got to one table," he said. "That's when we're at risk."

"Bat, Luke and Ben are all at the final table," Clark said. "Who's gonna try to steal the money with them and you still involved?"

Clint turned and faced Clark. "Someone interested in that kind of reputation. Come on, let's go."

THIRTY-NINE

Clint wiped the sleep from his eyes as he came out of John Ordway's room, then washed it from his mouth and throat with a beer before going into the poker room.

The six players were hard at it, stacks of chips all around. It was a remarkably evenly matched group of players, but Clint still felt the advantage had to go to Bat or Luke.

Ordway, Clark, Horne and Clint were all watching the game now. The only ones not watching were the bartender, Dillon, and the one girl who was working at the moment, Trudy. They were out by the temporary bar.

"You look a lot better," Horne said. "That nap took the edge off, huh?"

"I feel better," Clint said. "What about you?"

"I might go down for a couple of hours myself."

"Want me to ask Ordway if you can use his room?" Clint asked.

"No," Horne said, "I'll go and use my own room at the hotel. I'll see you in a few hours."

"Okay."

Horne left the room and went downstairs. Clint sidled

175

up next to Ordway and handed him back his keys.

"Thanks, it really helped."

"No problem," Ordway said, pocketing the key. "Look at this setup. Who do you think is going to win?"

"If I was betting I'd put my money on Bat or Luke," Clint admitted.

"I'll tell you who's surprising me," Clark said, joining them. "Slim Johnson. He doesn't even look like he can sit up, but his chip count is right up there with Bat's and Luke's."

"Looks like the next one out might be Thompson," Ordway said. "He's had a brutal run of luck with the cards. Even when he gets a good hand he's been gettin' beat."

Right at that moment Thompson called a bet with aces and sixes and lost to aces and tens. He sat back, shook his head, and fiddled with his dwindling stack of chips.

As they watched, two aces fell in front of Thompson and he did what anyone would do—he played them. In the end he pushed all his chips in against a pair of sixes on the table in front of Lucky Slim, who ended up winning with three sixes.

Ben Thompson stood up, shook hands with the other players at the table, and left the room with a wave to Clint.

As Thompson left the saloon, Catcher signaled to Dennis to come to the bar for a beer.

"That was Ben Thompson," he said. "That leaves five players, Masterson and Short among them."

"Do you want to wait for them to leave?"

"No," Catcher said, "I want to do it while they're there."

"But . . . Masterson and Short are deadly—"

"They've got the bigger reps," Catcher said, "but

Thompson is better with a gun than both of them."

"What?"

"That's right," Catcher said. "Even Masterson has said that Thompson's the deadliest man he's ever seen with a gun."

"What about Adams?"

"It's Thompson who would kill without a thought," Catcher said, "and he's gone."

"So what are you going to do?"

"I'm going up," Catcher said. "You and your partner cover me—and don't mess up."

"Are you sticking to the plan?' Dennis asked.

"Yeah," Catcher said, "I'm sticking to the plan."

Clint watched as the dealer fed the cards to the players. Slim had taken Ben Thompson down and now he seemed to have his sights set on Canadian Jack.

"Mr. Jack's play," the dealer said.

All five cards were on the table. Slim had a two, three, four, and five in front of him in mixed suits. He needed an ace or a six for a straight. Jack was high on the table, though, with a pair of kings.

"I'm all in," Jack said, pushing his chips in.

Slim wasted no time saying, "Call."

Jack turned over a third king, followed by Slim's ace. He had the straight and Canadian Jack was out of the game.

Jack shook hands all around, then shook hands with Clark and Ordway before heading out the door. Just seconds later, though, he came back through the door, staggering backward and then fell to the floor, unconscious.

"What the hell—" Ordway said.

Dillon came in then, and behind him a man holding a gun on him.

"Where did he come from?" Clint demanded.

"He came up the back stairs."

Clint looked at Ordway.

"The back stairs are blocked off."

"No very well, I'm afraid," Catcher said.

"Who are you?"

"Arlo Catcher's the name."

"I've heard of you."

"Good," Catcher said. "Lots more people will hear of me, too, after this. Now, everyone at the table keep your hands flat where I can see them."

Clint watched the players, figuring Bat was the one thinking about going for his gun. He was satisfied, though, when his friend put his hands on the table with everyone else's.

"Bartender," Catcher said, "collect everyone's gun— starting with Mr. Adams."

"W-what do I do with them?" Dillon asked.

"Toss them on one of those other tables."

Dillon approached Clint and seemed afraid to take the gun from his holster.

"Go ahead," Clint said, "take it."

Dillon removed it, then tossed it over on a table. Quickly, he relieved Dick Clark and John Ordway of their guns, also placing them on the table. After that he went around the table, relieving each gambler of his firearm and putting them on the table, which was now full of guns.

"Ben," Catcher said, "take one."

Dillon retrieved one gun from the table and said to Catch, "Look, Arlo, I've got the Gunsmith's gun."

He turned then and pointed the gun at the other men in the room, backing up to stand next to Arlo Catcher.

"You son of a bitch!" Ordway said.

"Sorry, boss," Dillon said, "but you don't pay very well, you know—at least, not anything that matches what's in that safe."

"Oh, yeah," Catcher said, "Mr. Ordway, would you be kind enough to open the safe?"

"You fellas aren't gonna get away with this," Bat said.

"Oh no?" Catcher asked. "Is the great Bat Masterson gonna stop us with his hands flat on the table?"

"You're not getting out of town with that money," Luke Short said.

"Watch me." Catcher pointed the gun directly at Ordway. "Open the damn safe!"

"Better do it, John," Clint said. "He'll kill you."

"He won't kill me," Ordway said. "I'm the only one who can open the safe."

"But if you refuse," Catcher said, "I might as well kill you, anyway, for all the good you'll do me."

"Open it, John," Clint said.

Ordway looked at Clint and said, "You were supposed to keep this from happening."

As Ordway bent down to open the safe Clint said, "It hasn't happened yet."

FORTY

"This is a big job for you, Catcher," Clint said. "Lots of money, lots of reps in the room. A little out of your league, isn't it?"

"What do you mean?"

"I mean I haven't heard of you doing anything this big before," Clint said. "I'm wondering who planned this, who you're working for."

"What makes you think I needed someone to plan this?" Catcher asked.

"Come on, Arlo," Clint said. "Admit it. You were brought into this last. Dillon's been in place for a while. I'll bet the brains is somebody here in town."

"Like who?" Catcher asked. "Don't you have that open yet?" he shouted at Ordway.

"It's a new combination," Ordway said. "I'll get it."

"What are you getting at, Clint?" Dick Clark asked. "Who do you suspect of planning this?"

It wasn't Clark's attention Clint had been trying to get, but Catcher's.

"Somebody who's been in town a while," Clint said, looking at Catcher, not Clark.

"Are you thinking I'm having my own game taken off?" Clark demanded.

"Relax, Dick," Bat said. "That's not what he's saying."

"Easy, Dick," Luke said.

"Come on, come on," Catcher said. "Get that safe open."

"You getting paid enough for this, Ben?" Clint asked.

"I'm gettin' paid plenty," Dillon said. "Don't worry about it. Mr. Brown pays very well."

"Dillon!" Catcher snapped.

"Ah, Mr. Brown," Clint said. "He's the boss?"

There was a moment of silence, and in that moment the safe clicked open audibly.

"It's open," Ordway said.

"Get the money out," Catcher said. "Put it in something."

"What?" Ordway asked.

"A bag," Catcher said. "Something. Wait!"

"Now what?' Ordway asked.

"Get away from the safe."

Ordway backed away.

"Ben, check and see if there's a gun in the safe."

Dillon moved toward the safe to take a look inside. As he did he passed between Catcher and Clint. At that moment Clint reached into his shirt for the little Colt New Line. As he came out with it, Catcher saw him. His gun had been pointed in the general direction of the men at the poker table. He started to bring it to bear on Clint but it was too late. Clint fired and his bullet took Catcher right in the chest, just above the heart. At that same moment Dillon looked around and Bat leaped at him from the table, grabbing his gun hand. They struggled and before anyone else could move, the gun went off. Bat cried out and staggered back, red blooming on his shirt front. Clint turned and fired again, this time hitting Dillon in the side of the head.

The doctor saw to Bat in Ordway's room, where they'd carried him and laid him on the bed.

"Damn fool thing to do," Clint said to his friend.

"Couldn't let you have all the glory, could I?" Bat asked.

Clint, Luke and the doctor were around the bed. The others were waiting outside the room.

"How is he, Doc?" Clint asked.

The sixty-ish sawbones finished applying a bandage to Bat's side and stood up.

"He'll be okay, but he's got to stay in bed for a while."

"Can't, Doc," Bat said. "I've got some money to win."

"Not today, you don't," the Doc said. "You'll keel over dead at the table before the game is over. You're out of the game, unless somebody plays for you."

Bat and Luke both looked at Clint.

"Hey, not me," Clint said. "I've got to find this Mr. Brown who planned this robbery—"

"No, you don't," Luke said. "Before he died, Catcher gave him up."

"Who is it?" Clint asked.

"O'Brien."

"Old man O'Brien?" Clint asked. "The one with the café?"

"The same."

"No wonder he was donating meals," Clint said. "He was checking out the setup whenever he came up here."

"He's probably not going anywhere," Luke said. "You can get him when the game's over. And even if he leaves town . . . so what?"

"There ya go," Bat said. "You've got to play for me,

Clint. I don't trust anybody else with my money. Besides, you owe me. I got shot trying to help you."

"Help me?" Clint said. "You were trying to save the prize money!"

"Which you were being paid to protect."

"Come on," Luke said to Clint. "We've got to get the game going before they disqualify Bat and me."

"Oh, all right," Clint said. "But if I lose—"

"If you lose it'll be because you didn't get the cards," Bat said, "or somebody outplayed you. Either way it could have happened to me, too. Just do your best."

"Okay," Clint said, "but you get some rest."

"Fine," Bat said. "I'm feeling a bit tired, anyway."

As Clint, Luke and the doctor walked out, Clint asked, "You think Dick and Ordway will let me play?"

"Dick kind of lost it in there when he thought you were accusing him," Luke said. "He'll let you play."

And he did. Ordway and Dick Clark agreed to allow Clint to fill in for Bat, as long as no one else at the table objected.

And no one did.

FORTY-ONE

"And Bat's not mad at you?" Andy asked Clint two days later. They were in his hotel room, in bed, a light coating of sweat covering them both. The game was over, the players had all left town, and Clint had spent the better part of two days in bed, either sleeping, or fucking Andy.

"What's he got to be mad at me about?" Clint asked, sliding a hand around her and cupping one chubby breast.

"Tell me again what happened." she said.

"I've told you twice . . . oh, all right . . ."

Clint sat down in Bat's chair and suddenly the cards started coming to him. Canadian Jack had left the room with nothing worse than a headache from where Catcher had struck him with his gun. That left Clint, Luke, John McNee and Lucky Slim in the game. The bets got bigger when Clint sat down, as if they were all trying to get this thing over with before someone else tried to rob the safe.

Clint took John McNee down, beating the man's three jacks with three queens of his own. McNee shook hands all around and left, and it was down to three for the money. The chip count looked even on the table, and all three men caught a hand that was not only playable but was, at most times, a winning hand.

But there could only be one winning hand.

Clint had three nines on the table.

Luke had the amazing luck to have amassed four eights, all on the table.

And Lucky Slim was showing a four, five, six and seven of hearts. He couldn't have an eight of hearts in the hole, because Luke already had it. The only thing that could beat Luke's four eights for him was the three of hearts.

What neither player knew was that Clint already had Luke beat with a fourth nine in the hole.

Luke said, "I've got no choice but to go all in with this hand."

And who could blame him?

Lucky Slim called.

Clint could have sat the hand out and still had money to play the winner, but good God, he had four nines. He had Luke Short's four eights beat.

"I call, as well," he said, pushing all his chips in.

"You're seein', gents," Luke Short said. "If you can beat four eights you deserve to win this game."

He was looking at Clint when he said it.

"I'm sorry, Luke," Clint said to his friend, and turned over the fourth nine.

Dick Clark, Art Home and John Ordway all gasped.

"Sonofabitch," Luke swore. "That's a bad beat."

"No," Lucky Slim wheezed, turning over a three of hearts for his straight flush, "this is."

"And a straight flush beats four of a kind?" Andy asked.

"Every time."

"And Bat wasn't mad?"

"Bat would have played it the same way."

"B-but . . . you lost over a million and a half dollars!"

"No, I didn't," he said. He rolled her over so that he was on top of her. Her big breasts flattened against her chest, the nipples the color of pennies. He could feel her pubic hair rubbing against him and he was already getting hard again.

"I only lost ten thousand dollars," he said, the tip of his penis probing her, "and Bat Masterson's ten thousand, at that!"

Watch for

IN FOR A POUND

271st novel in the exciting GUNSMITH
series from Jove

Coming in July!